Regency Morning
Elizabeth Law

ZEBRA BOOKS
KENSINGTON PUBLISHING CORP.

ZEBRA BOOKS

are published by

Kensington Publishing Corp.
475 Park Avenue South
New York, NY 10016

Copyright © 1988 by Maureen Peters. Published by arrangement with Walker and Company.

All rights reserved. No part of this book may be reproduced in any form or by any means without the prior written consent of the Publisher, exccpting brief quotes used in reviews.

First Zebra Books printing: October, 1990

Printed in the United States of America

= 1 =

THE ST. JOHN sisters sat in a neat row along the wall and gazed out over the meadows with varying degrees of gloom. A stranger, pausing to look at them, might not have realised they were sisters, so different were they in colouring and feature.

Laurie, the eldest, looked older than her eighteen years—her brown hair drawn back into an unfashionable bun, a worry crease etched between her eyes. Dora, who was seventeen, was by contrast distractingly pretty—her fair curls modishly short, her complexion of that particular tint generally described as blooming. Sixteen-year-old Clarisse was burdened with red hair and freckles, which bothered her not at all since she had no intention of ever marrying. All of them, however, had grey eyes, though these varied in shade from Laurie's clear silvery grey through Dora's blue-grey to Clarisse's darker orbs ringed in green round the iris.

As usual, it was Clarisse who broke the silence first.

"We could murder him," she said.

"We'd be found out and arrested and hanged," Dora said, her gloom unabated.

"Apart from which it would be illegal, I suppose," Clarisse allowed.

"And morally reprehensible," Laurie added severely.

"It was morally—what you just said—for Grandfather to entail the estate the way he did," Dora protested.

"He expected Papa and Mama to have sons," said

Laurie.

"Perhaps one of us could dress up and pretend to be a boy," said Clarisse.

"We are already known to be females," Laurie pointed out.

"There might have been a mistake," argued Clarisse. "Remember that kitten we called Prinny after the Prince of Wales? It had a litter before we realised."

"Cats are different," said Dora with an air of superior knowledge.

"We could make the murder look like an accident, I suppose," Clarisse mused.

"We could do nothing of the kind! I don't want to hear one more word about killing." Laurie was cross now. "Let us keep within the bounds of possibility."

"It is within the bounds of possibility that he might be waylaid and shot by footpads on the way here," Dora said.

Laurie considered a moment, despite her crossness, then shook her head. "From what I've heard," she said, "Cousin Tarquin is more likely to do the shooting."

From the spire at the far side of the meadows a chime of church bells gladdened the wind. Clarisse, who was going through an intensely religious phase when she was not contemplating murder, immediately slid from the low wall onto her knees.

"Oh, do get up, Clary," Dora begged. "Someone might see."

"Joan of Arc always knelt down when she heard the Angelus ring," Clarisse said.

"Joan of Arc was French, and the French have very strange habits," Dora said. "Think of Napoleon."

It was only four years since the Battle of Waterloo had removed the Corsican monster from the nightmares of English children, so the three girls were silent for a moment. Then Laurie added in her usual practical tone, "Anyway it isn't the Angelus. It's only Mr. Phillips testing the new bell."

"Isn't Cousin Tarquin's mother French?" Clarisse asked, scrambling up from her knees.

"An *emigré*," Laurie nodded. "Uncle Tarquin married her to save her from the guillotine."

"What a pity!" Dora sighed. "If he had left her to her fate there wouldn't be any Cousin Tarquin to turn us out of our ancestral home."

As if pulled by the same cord, the three youthful heads turned to look back over the wall towards the house which stood on a slight rise beyond the well-tended lawns and flower beds. This particular home was not exactly ancestral since it had been built by their grandfather and was less than a hundred years old, but it had already acquired the patina of age. Its walls were embraced by the clinging stems of ivy. Its windows looked out over the landscape as if they had been looking out that way for centuries. Seen at a little distance, the house had grace and dignity, but money had been scarce since Papa's last ill-fated speculation, and at close quarters one could discern the genteel shabbiness of the whole, with fresh white paint covering the cracked stone of the sills and much of the garden given over to vegetables.

When Laurence St. John built his estate, he intended it to become the showplace of the neighbourhood, and for a time it had been just that. However, the death of his wife after the birth of their third daughter rendered St. John dissatisfied with home life. From then on, he had spent most of his time in London, discussing the progress of the war with his cronies at White's and only occasionally descending upon Gables with presents for his motherless girls and an unfortunate tendency to muddle their names. His death from an untimely attack of grippe three months before this had been a sadness but not a tragedy. The real tragedy lay in the fact that Cousin Tarquin, the elder son of Laurence St. John's younger brother, had written politely to inform his three female cousins that he had returned from the Americas and intended to ride over and inspect his property.

"If only Papa had not waited until he was near forty before taking a wife," Dora sighed.

"Would we have been boys if he had married young?" enquired Clarisse.

"I don't think so." Dora, who was not at all sure, glanced at Laurie but her elder sister had retreated into one of her rare daydreaming periods, her grey eyes distracted as they gazed across the meadow.

"There's Mattie." Clarisse whisked through the gate as a plump figure appeared at the side of the house and waved vigorously. "It must be tea-time."

Neither fire, flood, nor the impending loss of her home could have led Clarisse to neglect her appetite, though she never put on an ounce of surplus flesh. Dora, on the other hand, was, for all her prettiness, inclined to be plump.

"Clarisse is such a child," she said now, watching the younger girl pick up her skirts and scamper up the path. "I am certain I couldn't eat a morsel."

Laurie made no answer. Dora, glancing sharply at her sister, saw that she had sunk deeper into her reverie. Occasionally, when these fits of abstraction overcame her, Laurie would go off to write a poem.

"Do you feel a poem coming on?" Dora asked anxiously.

"I need to think," Laurie answered at last. "Do go and eat your tea."

"I may," said Dora, sliding from her perch, "be able to manage the tiniest sliver of cake."

Laurie hardly noticed her sister's departure. Her mind was concentrated on the problem she had tried to avoid since her father's funeral. They had been living on borrowed time from then on, and Cousin Tarquin's letter brought them back to reality with a thud.

Penned in a bold flourishing hand, the message had been polite, formal, and irrevocable:

"My dear Cousin Laurentia,

Allow me to express my condolences on the recent death of your father. I was not able to attend the funeral as I did not arrive in England until all was over. I shall be travelling to Gables at the beginning of the next month as soon as I have consulted the family lawyers and look forward then to making your acquaintance again after my long sojourn abroad. Please convey my condolences to your sisters, Theodora and Clarisse,

>and believe me to be, Your Affectionate Cousin,
>Tarquin St. John."

It had been twelve years since he visited Gables for the first and, until now, the only time. Laurie had a vague recollection of a very dark boy who had looked down at her from a great height and then gone on talking to Papa. She had been six then and very worried about two loose front teeth, which mercifully remained in her mouth until after the visitor had departed, when Mattie had tied cotton to them and banged the barn door shut to make them fly out quickly.

Laurie had no memory of her cousin's departure and had given him scarcely a thought in the intervening time. For her, as for most children, her father had seemed invested with an aura of immortality. His death had caused more surprise than genuine grief, especially since, though he had never been harsh, she knew that he would have preferred her to be a boy. Dora was so pretty that nobody would have wanted to change her sex, and the sad circumstances of Clarisse's birth—with poor Mama dying two weeks later—had caused Laurence St. John to regard his youngest daughter with melancholy affection. It was too bad that his younger brother, Tarquin, had married young and produced two sons. As the estate was entailed through the male heirs of the elder son, Laurie would have cut out both her older cousins had she not been a female. It was simply too provoking that she had been doomed to wear skirts.

Her grey eyes, described by Mattie with insensitive but not spiteful candour as her one beauty, sharpened into awareness again as Laurie gazed towards the house. Her sisters never noticed its flaws, but Laurie was not so blind to its shabbiness, which had increased over the years as her father's investments failed and the cost of living rose. It was a beautiful house—with twin columns at each side of the front door, mullioned windows, curving staircase—but it needed money spending. The roof leaked in several places, and the family portraits were stained by patches of damp.

She wondered if Cousin Tarquin might be rich. If so, then he would certainly spend on the restoration of his own property.

Her grandfather had been wealthy following involvement with the East India Company, wealthy enough to provide both his sons with handsome legacies. The younger had followed him into the Company, but the elder preferred more risky speculations. There was little compatibility between the brothers, and Uncle Tarquin had been killed in a riding accident some years before when both his sons were past the age of requiring schooling. Laurie tried to recall exactly what her father had said of them.

"More like me than their father. Poor old Tarquin was always a bit of a sobersides. The elder lad went off to the Americas to find adventure, though with old Boney rattling round Europe he could have found it nearer to home. The younger, Simon, has a minor post at Court. Lives with his mother somewhere or other in London."

Though Laurence St. John spent most of his time in the capital, it had apparently not occurred to him to pay his respects to his widowed sister-in-law, and Cousin Tarquin's one brief visit to Gables had never been repeated. There was no open estrangement between the two sides of the family, more an embarrassment due to the terms of the entail. Now, however, Papa was most inconsiderately dead, and Grandfather's will would come into effect. Cousin Tarquin was on the way to inspect his inheritance, and unless Laurie thought of something very quickly she and her sisters would be without a home.

They were not entirely without money, since her father had willed his fortune in three equal parts to his daughters. Unfortunately, that fortune had been whittled away by unwise speculation over the years, and what remained would yield only a modest annual income.

Laurie turned from her distressing thoughts. Mattie was coming down from the garden path with scolding in her face and concern in her voice. "Sitting on cold stone gives one the rheumatics quicker than anything I know. Do come and get your tea, Miss Laurie."

"Save some for me," said Laurie, jumping down from her perch. "I'm going to church."

"At tea-time? With no service going on?" Mattie looked as shocked as if Laurie had announced she was going to a gaming den. "You're not getting religion like Miss Clarisse, are you?" Mattie asked anxiously. She had nothing against religion herself, of course, provided it was confined to Sundays and not talked about in company.

"I'll only be half an hour," said Laurie and, to forestall further protest, set off rapidly across the meadow.

It was a beautiful afternoon with the shadows only just starting to lengthen over the tangled, sunlit grass. The gentle breeze swayed the tops of the elm trees in the lane. Laurie's black dress looked out of place among the meadowsweet and poppies that raised defiant heads from the corn field beyond the churchyard. Mourning suited some colourings—Dora's for instance—but it did absolutely nothing for Laurie's light brown hair and paleness. Her appearance was the farthest thing from her mind, however, as she pushed open the gate and walked up the path with its border of scallop shells. She had long since come to terms with the fact that she lacked Dora's beauty and Clarisse's vivacity.

Mr. Phillips had gone and the church was empty. It was an old church. Its foundations were reputed to be Saxon though its superstructure was Norman. Generations of villagers had lived their lives within this parish—dipped in the font when they were squealing babies, making their marriage vows within its doors, occupying first low benches, then high-backed pews through a thousand sermons, and finally being laid to rest within the graveyard at the side.

In Tudor times, the gold and silver had been seized by a rapacious king. During the Civil War, the altar and stained glass windows were dismantled and hidden until the king came into his own again. More recently, a brass plate had been affixed to the nave bearing the names of six local men who had died at Trafalgar and Waterloo.

Laurie had always loved the old church and the sense of timelessness she felt within its walls. She sat down now in a pew near the side altar and closed her eyes, not praying exactly, but opening herself to whatever brilliant idea the Lord might see fit to send. Instead, there came an opening and closing of the door and an impatient voice saying, "Is there anybody here or is the entire neighbourhood under a spell?"

"The entire neighbourhood is having tea," said Laurie, rising and turning to face the intruder.

"Except yourself." He moved further into the church, limping as he did so. He was a tall man, face in shadow, voice brusque.

"And you," she pointed out. "Are you hurt, sir?"

"A sprain, no worse. My wretched horse threw me and galloped off. The attractions of a pretty mare in the field, I suspect. After so long a ride I'm astonished that he had the energy or inclination. I rang at the vicarage but without result."

"The vicar will be over at the school giving scripture class. Do you require someone to catch your horse?"

"Pedro will find me when he's a mind." The voice

sounded less brusque now. A careless good humour had crept into it. "I require directions. I am on my way to the Gables."

"Ah, then you rode into the village from the southern path. If you had turned left at the old barn you would have come directly to the—You must be Cousin Tarquin!"

"And you must be one of Uncle Laurence's daughters?"

"I am Laurie—Laurentia."

She stepped closer, peering up at his face in the uncertain light. He was still black-browed and dark-haired, but there was nothing boyish in his harsh, saturnine features. His nose jutted above a mouth firm to the point of tightness. His jawline was visibly obstinate.

"You've grown," he said after a moment's pause.

"In twelve years one usually does." She felt a pang of disappointment. Whatever else she had been expecting, it wasn't stupidity.

"I suppose so. I merely made the expected and conventional comment. So you are Laurentia?"

"I'm called Laurie," she volunteered. "My sisters—"

"Dora and Clary, I suppose."

"Dora and Clarisse. She prefers the full version of her name though occasionally it is shortened."

Why they were talking rubbish about names she couldn't imagine, unless it was to fill the silence caused by surprise and uneasiness.

"Do I interrupt your devotions?" he asked politely.

"No, I was just sitting," she said and passed through the door he held open for her. The sunshine struck her sharply after the gloom of the church, and she shaded her eyes with her hand. He limped after and peered down at her from his greater height with the air of impatience she had noticed at first.

"I believe I am correct in thinking my visit inopportune," he said abruptly. "I am aware of how difficult the situation must be for you."

"You mistake, Cousin Tarquin." Her tone was cooler now, as the shock of his sudden appearance waned. "We have always known that one day you would come."

"Like the Day of Judgement, you mean?" A faint quirk arched the corners of his well-shaped mouth.

"I hope neither so final nor so devastating," Laurie responded. "Shall I seek assistance for you? Your ankle must pain you."

"It will wear off. I'm no lover of the medical fraternity. Where is Uncle Laurence buried?"

"Over there." She indicated the railed plot where their mutual grandparents, her mother, and, more recently, her father had been laid.

Cousin Tarquin limped to the graves and stood, dark head bowed, in what she took to be a sop to the conventions.

"I don't remember my grandparents," he said when he rejoined her, "but I liked Uncle Laurence on the rare occasions we met. He more than once stood between me and my father in an argument."

"You were on bad terms with your father?"

"Not all the time." He flashed a wry smile which lit the darkness of his features. "I was very attached to him, as a matter of fact, but like most parents he hoped for perfection in his offspring. I went through the usual period of wild-oat sowing which a man with more perception might have taken in his stride. Father did not. Uncle Laurence stood up for me, and eventually made the splendid suggestion that I try my luck in the Americas to satisfy my craving for adventure."

"Perhaps he hoped you'd be killed out there," Laurie said before she could stop herself. She clapped her hand over her mouth, but the damage was done.

Her cousin gave her a hard look and replied, "I fear you attribute your own wishes to your father. Uncle Laurence was not a man of vengeful spirit, I assure you. Besides, if anything had happened to me there is still my younger brother, Simon. Thus, my demise would have been wasted."

Laurie bit her lip and walked on, accommodating her

pace to his limp.

"Here is Pedro, fresh from his lovemaking." Tarquin's voice lifted as a big bay stallion cantered up the lane. "Bad boy. Cousin, if you will allow me the use of your shoulder, I can mount and ride on."

He would be at the house long before she could run through the meadows to warn them of his arrival. Laurie racked her brain for a solution as he grasped her shoulder and mounted with surprising agility for a tall, heavily built man. He gathered up the reins and looked down at her.

"Let us be frank with each other," he said. "I am well aware that my coming is not a matter for rejoicing on your part. In your position, I would feel considerable resentment. However, with a little goodwill on both sides, I believe we can settle matters to our mutual satisfaction."

Laurie watched silently as he wheeled his mount around and set off at a brisk trot down the lane. She could see that Cousin Tarquin was a man who knew his own mind and would brook no interference in any plans he chose to make. He was also handsome, in a dour way, and not entirely without humour.

The idea which had been growing in her mind began to flower as she stepped over the narrow ditch that separated lane from meadow and walked towards the house. There was no point in running to arrive breathless and untidy.

As Laurie neared the garden wall, Dora flitted out to meet her. She began talking before she had reached her sister's side. "Cousin Tarquin is here. He said he met you in the church. His horse threw him and he is having a cold compress put on his ankle. He is very handsome, don't you think? But very stern with those black eyes!"

"He seems a gentleman," Laurie admitted. "He is sensible of the embarrassment his arrival causes. Who is entertaining him?"

"He told Mattie to bring him something stronger than

tea. She went without argument, which is most unusual for her. He has a way of speaking as if he expected to be obeyed."

"And has begun to issue orders already." Laurie shrugged and hastened her step. "I had better make certain the guest room is fit to be seen. Dora, you see that he has everything he wants. You are always good at making casual conversation."

And so enchantingly pretty, thought Laurie. He will be sure to fall in love with you, which means that one of us at least won't be forced to leave Gables. The prospect of Dora's marriage cheered Laurie so much she hummed under her breath as she went up the path. Dora lagged behind, still trying to accustom herself to the reality of their cousin's arrival, just as Clarisse emerged from a side door, a last piece of cake still in her fingers.

"What did Laurie say?" she asked.

"That he seemed like a gentleman."

"Nothing more?" Clarisse looked disappointed, then brightened. "Well, Laurie never was one to enthuse about anything. In my opinion they will suit each other very well."

"She has never talked of marrying," said Dora.

"There isn't anybody worth marrying roundabout here," Clarisse said. "Besides, Laurie is practical. She will want to keep Gables, so she will do the right thing. I only hope that Cousin Tarquin falls in love with her quite quickly. I do hate suspense."

= 2 =

ENTERING THE HOUSE, Laurie hesitated and then went into the drawing room, where she guessed Mattie had taken her cousin. He was there all right, his sprained ankle resting on a footstool, a decanter of brandy on the small table at his elbow.

"Forgive my not rising, Cousin," he said, turning his head as Laurie came in. "My foot is rather more swollen than I had realised. This is excellent brandy."

"Papa always thought so," Laurie said coldly.

She had meant to be pleasant, but the sight of him seated in the chair where her father had usually sat on the rare occasions he was at Gables irritated her. Cousin Tarquin had lost no time in making himself at home.

"Mattie recommended it," he said.

"Mattie?" Laurie's delicate eyebrows shot upward before she remembered that Mattie too had met him before and so probably wouldn't object to the use of her nickname.

"We usually have supper at seven, country hours. If you want anything changed—"

"Country hours are fine," he assured her. "I don't expect you to change everything merely because I'm here."

"But things will inevitably change." She sat down on a low-backed chair and folded her hands in the lap of her black gown. "We have known that ever since Papa died."

"I am not here to turn your lives upside down," Cousin Tarquin answered with a trace of impatience. "I propose to stay for a few days until we have worked out some arrangement congenial to us all."

"We have been making plans ourselves. Fortunately, we are all three of us far from being destitute. Papa left us well provided."

"I am relieved to hear it," he said gravely. "I wouldn't like to think of your being a charge on the parish."

Laurie glanced at him sharply. He was sipping his brandy, and his expression was serious.

"Do you wish to see the papers and documents now?" she asked formally. "I have the keys to Papa's desk and the safe box, though I think most of the important documents are in London at the lawyer's chambers."

"I have seen those, and there is no great hurry for the rest." He set down the glass and gave her a faint smile. "I propose to be unsociable this evening and have a tray sent up to my room. It was a long ride and my foot causes me some discomfort."

"Perhaps it is broken. Shall I send for the doctor?" She was moved to some compunction, noticing that he winced as he moved.

"I promise you it is no more than a bad sprain. By morning it will be immeasurably improved. Then you can show me round, and we will discuss what's best to be done."

"I think you would find Dora a more interesting guide than myself," Laurie seized the opportunity to say. "She knows so many quaint legends about the district."

"Which I shall be happy to hear on another occasion. Shall we say ten o'clock?"

"As you please, Cousin." Temper seethed inside her at his calm assumption of authority, but she contrived to answer him politely. "I will tell Mattie that you require a supper tray."

Somehow or other she left the room without banging the door and ran up the stairs to the large chamber which had originally been the nursery and now served as an informal sitting room for the girls. Her sisters were already there. Dora sat in the window seat, where the setting sun haloed her hair. Some unkind people might suspect she was well aware of the charming picture she made, but in fact Dora arranged herself to the best advantage without thinking about it. Clarisse toasted a bun at the fire, unashamed of the hearty tea she had just eaten.

"You look miffed," she observed, turning a flushed face towards her eldest sister.

"I find Cousin Tarquin a trifle high-handed," Laurie began crossly.

"He has very long eyelashes," Dora said.

"What has the length of his eyelashes to do with anything?" Laurie broke off sharply, remembering her plans for Dora. She went on more calmly. "I expect I am being rather foolish. Certainly he seems concerned not to upset us. Perhaps his wanting a tray in his room is his way of being tactful on his first evening here. And his ankle is hurting him. It is the entire situation that is so difficult."

"Does he mean to turn us out?" Clarisse enquired, blowing on the scorched bun.

"I doubt if that is in his mind," Laurie admitted. "He wishes to come to some arrangement, but naturally we are all too proud to accept a roof out of charity."

"Are we?" Dora caught Laurie's stern look and amended it to, "We are indeed!"

"In the morning Dora can show him round," Laurie was continuing, but Dora broke in, "You're the eldest and ought to do the honours, Laurie. He's visited Gables before. He surely knows the way everywhere already."

"He had forgotten the turning at the crossroads," Laurie said.

"If he wishes to know about the cost of things and when the roof was last mended, I will be sure to muddle myself," Dora argued.

Laurie hesitated and then shrugged. It made little difference who played hostess. Over the next few days she would contrive to have Cousin Tarquin and Dora thrown regularly into each other's company.

"What is going to happen?" Clarisse asked with the

faintest quiver in her voice, reminding the older girls that she was only just past sixteen and had been Papa's favourite.

"Nothing very terrible," Laurie said quickly. "We are each of us possessed of an income, and can easily find a comfortable house where we may live together."

She hoped silently that comfortable houses were available at the rent they would be able to pay. If Tarquin fell in love with Dora, then there would be only herself and Clarisse to settle. Mattie could go with them to keep house and they would get along splendidly, Laurie reassured herself, but, to her dismay, she felt tears welling up in her eyes. She hastily left the room, murmuring something about seeing to their cousin's tray.

"Would you say she is taken with him?" Clarisse asked, munching the toasted bun.

"Laurie never displays her feelings," said Dora, "but she did appear remarkably out of humour when she came in. I'd take that for a hopeful sign."

"When she does marry him, what will you do? I intend to become a nun, but I don't suppose you'd want that."

Dora, who could think of nothing she would like less, shuddered, but, being a kind-hearted girl said merely, "Oh, I expect someone or other will fall in love with me. They generally do." She spoke the plain truth. Her large grey-blue eyes and bewitching blonde curls reduced most males to helpless infatuation while Dora, who regarded her looks as a fortunate accident of nature, smiled benignly upon her suitors and giggled about them later.

Laurie had fled to the kitchen, where it was always possible to find refuge even in the worst times. Next to the old nursery, the kitchen was her favourite part of the house. It was at the back where Mattie could keep a stern eye on the vegetable plot and the comings and goings of tradesmen and errand boys. Potted herbs ranged the sills of the long windows which looked out across the back garden towards the stables. Laurence St. John had sold off all the horses except Daisy, who was ridden in turn by his daughters, and the only male servant now employed, apart from the gardener, was the boot boy, who slept in a cubbyhole under the stairs and squabbled mightily with the tweeny. Two girls from the village comprised the rest of the current domestic staff, but Mattie could remember a time when there had been a butler, two footmen, and a coachman. She ruled now over a diminished empire but she ruled nevertheless—her dignity unimpaired.

"I've some of the peach pie left, which is a mercy," she announced as Laurie entered.

"Cousin Tarquin wants a tray in his room."

"Yes, I know. In my opinion he ought to have that ankle looked at, but he won't hear of it. He was always stubborn, even as a boy. Do you think he'd fancy chicken or turkey? Perhaps I'd better put both."

"Why not the fatted calf?" asked Laurie, disappointment making her sharp.

"Now don't be quoting the Good Book on a weekday," Mattie said, her eyes roaming over the tray. "The pickles are about ready, which is a mercy, for chicken goes wonderfully well with a few sharp pickles. Would you step over and give the soup a stir, Miss Laurie? It seems such a long time since we had a male appetite in this house that I'm sure we haven't provided half enough."

Laurie had hoped for consolation and found treason instead. She gave the bubbling soup a cursory stir then went to the window, where she pulled off a thin shoot of rosemary and crumbled it in her fingers.

"Did you recognise him straight off?" she asked.

"The minute I laid eyes on him," said Mattie, spearing pickles out of a jar. "He's very much like poor Mr. Laurence when he was younger, but taller."

"He will require to see everything, I suppose."

"All is in order," Mattie said with satisfaction, "and he'll see the work that needs doing soon enough, I daresay. It will be a relief to have a man in charge again. Not that you don't do your best, Miss Laurie, but you haven't had the experience it takes to run an estate."

She spoke as if Laurence St. John had been the most efficient of employers, though he'd paid the bills as rarely as he could get away with, and never noticed cracked panes and leaking pipes.

"Papa always gave me to understand that Cousin Tarquin was rather a wild young boy," Laurie said, "but he strikes me as serious."

"Boys grow into men, and I daresay he had his fill of adventure when he was in America. Do stop pulling that plant apart, Miss Laurie."

It obviously hadn't occurred to Mattie that they were all now dependent on Cousin Tarquin for their home. Laurie sighed and wandered out of the kitchen, more restless than she had been since her father's death. Her cousin had evidently retired to the guest room, since the drawing room was deserted. She went through to the parlour and took up her sewing. Her fingers flew while her thoughts remained sadly discomposed.

Later on, at dinner—by which name she had better learn to call supper in future, Laurie supposed—the girls were silent, each wrapped in her own thoughts, but that didn't prevent Clarisse from taking second helpings.

The door of the guest room was closed when Laurie went past on the way to her room. She had a chamber of her own to mark her place as the eldest in the family, whereas Dora and Clarisse slept together, snuggled in a double bed under a down quilt. Laurie sometimes felt a twinge of loneliness when she woke in the night, but this evening she was glad of her privacy. She needed to ponder without interruption.

Dora must marry Cousin Tarquin. He was handsome, Laurie admitted grudgingly, and his gravity would be a foil for Dora's lightness of heart. Laurie worried about Dora, knowing that along with her beauty went a constitutional inability to concentrate on anything serious for very long. Of the three sisters, she was most in need of a rich, adoring husband.

As for herself . . . Laurie plaited her hair, following her obligatory hundred strokes of the brush, and decided that she and Clarisse could manage very nicely in a small cottage. It was possible that Clarisse would enter an Anglican order. Then Laurie could set her cap for a clergyman or widower who didn't demand an enormous dowry or a high degree of beauty.

She found herself wondering, before dropping off to sleep, why the future she had mapped out for herself didn't please her more.

In the morning, the prospect looked brighter. Laurie drank the coffee Mattie brought up and decided that the best course of action was to be very firm and very adult. She would make it clear to Cousin Tarquin that they had no intention of being a burden upon him.

There was no sign of him at breakfast when she went down. Bess, who was serving, volunteered the information that the gentleman had saddled up earlier and gone into the village. No doubt he wanted to renew his acquaintance with people he had met as a boy on holiday at Gables, thought Laurie. Certainly he seemed to be making himself at home without troubling to consult anyone else's wishes.

He was back before ten. All three sisters heard his voice in the yard, and a moment later he came in, still limping but obviously in less pain than on the previous day. Dora was the first to greet him.

"Good morning," he responded from the open door, stripping off his gloves.

In the sunlight, his hair shone so black there was a tinge of blue to it. His skin was tanned in a way that might have marked him as less than a gentleman had it not been for the immaculate riding clothes and lacy cravat.

"Would you like some breakfast?" Clarisse asked politely. "I didn't eat everything."

"I breakfasted earlier. If you can spare me some time, however, cousins, we shall discuss future plans."

His tone was brisk and businesslike, devoid of sentiment or apology. Not that he needed to apologise for an entail made before he was born, Laurie reminded herself as she rose and led the way into the study. Still, he looked uncommonly cheerful at the prospect of taking over as master of Gables.

The study was the name given to the room where Laurence St. John had been accustomed to take his ease when he was at home, though he had been a student of nothing more taxing to the brain than racing forms and bloodlines. Nevertheless, there were books in the glass-fronted cases at each side of the high mantel and a pile of old sporting papers on the table. The three sisters seated themselves—Dora and Clarisse in armchairs, Laurie in a straight chair. Cousin Tarquin seated himself at the flat-topped desk, looking for all the world as if he had belonged there for years.

"I have the keys to the desk," Laurie said, laying them before him. "I believe that you will find the account books in order."

"I have no doubt about it, Cousin." He glanced at the keys without picking them up.

"Repairs are needed to the roof and the stables, but you probably noticed that for yourself."

"Those are mundane matters," he answered with some impatience. "Naturally, I'll do whatever is necessary to put my property in good repair. What concerns me more immediately is yourselves."

"Papa did provide for us," Laurie began defensively.

"To the amount of four hundred pounds a year, if I understood the lawyers correctly. That is hardly a fortune."

"We live very simply. We are not extravagant."

Dora heaved a gentle sigh as if, given the chance, she might be persuaded to a little extravagance. Clarisse commented more virtuously, "I am going to be a nun, so I shall divide my share between my sisters."

"As far as I can gather," he said, ignoring her contribution, "you have completed your formal education."

"More than a year ago. Miss Browne went to another post."

"But none of you has come out yet?"

"With our small income it seems rather inappropriate," Laurie said.

"And we don't much want to," Clarisse affirmed, pretending not to notice Dora's frown.

"All young ladies ought to have one Season," their cousin demurred. "At least that is what my mother says. She has no daughters of her own and is looking forward to the pleasure of chaperoning her nieces in Society."

Laurie privately doubted that, since their aunt had been conspicuous by her absence throughout their motherless childhood.

"Cousin Laurie and Cousin Dora can make their debuts together," he went on. "Next year it will be Cousin Clarisse's turn. Any necessary repairs and renovations to this house can be carried out while you are all in London."

"It costs money to launch oneself into Society," said Laurie.

"Fortunately, I am a reasonably wealthy man."

"No indeed!" In her agitation, Laurie had risen from her chair. "We could not possibly impose upon you."

"I consider it my duty, Cousin."

"You have no obligations at all as far as we are concerned," she insisted.

"That is not quite accurate. As your legal guardian I have certain responsibilities."

"Legal guardian? We don't have any guardian," said Dora, sounding a bit bewildered.

"It was not specified in the will," he agreed, "but by law your nearest male relative is your guardian until you reach the age of twenty-one."

Laurie sat down again abruptly and stared at him.

"Naturally," he continued, "I shall feel it incumbent on me to do what is necessary for your happiness and well-being."

"Surely, there is a legal loophole somewhere—," Laurie began.

"I see no point in searching for one," he broke in.

"You're too young to be a guardian," Dora exclaimed.

"I agree that the circumstances are unusual. However, I am not far short of thirty, and my mother will be able to act as duenna so your scruples are unnecessary. I will certainly do my best for all of you within my own financial limitations."

He sounded as pompous as a man of forty, Laurie thought. A spark of anger had kindled in her grey eyes. For as long as she could recall, she had been virtually her own mistress. Her father had spent most of his time in the city, and Miss Browne had been a gentle creature who regarded her charges as motherless chicks to be coaxed into as much education as they wished and disciplined hardly at all.

"We are still in mourning," Laurie reminded him. "Six months has not yet elapsed since Papa's death."

"I was thinking of launching you in a fairly modest manner," he said dryly. "My mother would be better qualified to advise you as to the correct colours that might be worn."

"Pale blue and coffee cream would look pretty," Dora said.

Laurie opened her mouth to rebuke her sister, then closed it again. If there had to be a launching into society, then the advantage might lie with Dora. She would look enchanting in garments suitable for balls and supper parties. Cousin Tarquin would fall madly in love with her and forget his tiresome sense of obligation towards herself and Clarisse.

Unfortunately, at the moment Cousin Tarquin didn't look capable of falling in love with anyone. He was a dull and humourless stick, in Laurie's opinion, even if he had gone roving to the other side of the world. Perhaps he'd done so merely to increase his fortune.

"I assume you'll want a few days to make your

farewells to the neighbours," he was saying, "and time to pack what you require."

"You wish us to travel to London so soon?" asked Laurie in dismay.

"The Season begins in less than a month. You will need to prepare."

His tone was mild, but she was beginning to guess at the depths of obstinacy that lay beneath. Laurie well understood that the only way to counter obstinacy was with meekness.

Lowering her eyes, she said, "We would like Mattie to accompany us."

"That will be for Mattie to decide." He softened his reply with a slight smile that she failed to see. "I will look through the account books and ride back to London tomorrow, then send the carriage for you at the beginning of the week."

Laurie opened her mouth to inform him that they had their own carriage but remembered in time that the springs in it had gone.

"If I'm not to be launched," said Clarisse, "why must I come to London?"

"To complete your education," he answered.

"But I already—"

"I know. You were already educated by the estimable Miss Browne. However, there are many interesting sights to be seen in the capital. If you are to renounce the world, you had better see as much of it as possible first."

Thus, without actually dismissing them, he had done so, and Laurie found herself leading the others out while their cousin bent his head over the account books he had taken from the desk drawer.

"Guardian!" Dora squealed as they reached the garden. "Had you any notion of it, Laurie?"

"It never entered my head," Laurie admitted. "Papa was always so sure he would live into old age that he seldom discussed what would become of us when he was gone."

"So we are to be bundled off to London and launched into Society. At least you are, while I am expected to improve my mind with sight-seeing trips," Clarisse said, not hiding her resentment.

"I'm certain he is well intentioned." Laurie was torn between indignation at the cool manner in which he had assumed command of their destinies and her reluctance to set Dora against him.

"We ought to have poisoned him," Clarisse declared. She sounded wistful.

3

THE PARTING FROM their home had had a different effect upon each of them. Clarisse reminded herself that when she became a nun she would have to rise above personal likings and regarded this first leave-taking as a preparation. Apart from that she was still young enough to regard any journey as an adventure, and the idea of London became less daunting the more she considered it. Dora also found herself secretly looking forward to the change. Although she was contented by nature, the prospect of entering Society didn't alarm her. She was aware, without being the least vain about it, that her beauty would serve as a passport wherever she chose to go.

It was upon Laurie that the leaving fell hardest. She had a deep and abiding love for Gables and the village. That love extended beyond conventional feeling for one's birthplace, and to depart from there was to leave part of herself behind. Had it not been for her hope that Dora, given a glamorous setting, would entice Cousin Tarquin more readily into matrimony, Laurie would have openly rebelled. Instead, she packed up what she would need during her stay in the city, visited the neighbours to receive their farewells and good wishes, then spent some time alone in walking through the meadows and along the banks of the river so that she could carry the picture of them inside her forever.

Cousin Tarquin had ridden away the day after the conversation in the study, returning the keys of the desk to her with the comment that he had found all the books in perfect order, just as he expected. He was very polite, and she had been equally so. When he had gone, she found herself wondering if Dora would be able to get past his cool, quiet exterior and waken whatever passion lay within.

Meanwhile, Mattie wasn't going with the girls, despite all their pleadings. "I was never in London in my born days, and I'm too old to travel there now," she said firmly. "I'd be out of my depth in a fine city house, and you're not children to be needing me any longer. If I leave Gables, who's to say that the workmen won't go spoiling more than they repair? I'll stay and keep an eye on things for you all."

She had made it sound as if she was prepared to defend Gables against the ravages of an invader instead of merely supervising a gang of craftsmen come to effect repairs long overdue.

"I don't know how we shall contrive without Mattie," Dora said sadly.

That there would be other servants in the London house was something none of them commented upon. Mattie was more than a servant. She was part of the fabric of their childhood. Her staying behind symbolised more than anything else the changes that were taking place.

As for their dress upon the journey, after much discussion they had decided to lay aside full mourning in favour of subdued shades of grey and lavender, though it flouted convention. Since Laurence St. John had cared not at all for the conventions, they trusted they were doing the right thing.

"Aunt would not enjoy having three sable crows foisted upon her," Laurie concluded.

"How can we tell what she will like?" Clarisse asked. "We have never met her."

"Her Christian name is Marie, and she escaped from

the guillotine and married Uncle Tarquin," Dora recited.

"We didn't know him either," Clarisse pointed out.

"As she is willing to launch us into polite society," Laurie said, aware of the faint irony in her voice, "we ought to begin by preparing ourselves to like her and do whatever is in our power to make her like us. Black garments may remind her of unhappiness she prefers to forget."

So it was grey and blue and cream for the St. John girls, still unrelieved by the frivolity of pink or yellow.

They had expected Cousin Tarquin to return with the carriage that was to take them to London. However, the gleaming vehicle with its four black horses which rolled up the drive to Gables carried only the coachman and his assistant.

It was certainly a very grand coach, and the sisters' spirits rose despite themselves. At least they would be leaving Gables and arriving in London in fine style.

The journey would take most of the day, though they would start soon after daybreak. Laurie had expected to find the actual parting a terrible wrench, but was spared by Mattie's suddenly dissolving into tears and crying out that it was the last time they would meet since she felt in her bones they would all three be murdered by footpads. When other people went to pieces, Laurie's own common sense came to the rescue.

"Nobody at all is going to be murdered," she said calmly. "The drivers are well armed, and we shall be travelling by day rather than in the middle of the night when such things happen. It is summer and the roads will be in excellent condition, so do cease fretting."

Mattie didn't exactly cease, but she wiped her eyes on her apron and fell to worrying over the nuncheon basket she had prepared. She had put in sufficient for the three of them and filled a second basket for the drivers, but was concerned that the jolting of the coach might curdle the pot of cream or crack the dishes.

Meanwhile, the luggage had been strapped on, and the

horses were champing at their bits. The sun had only just begun to rise, and there were still trailing shadows of darkness over the garden. It was easier to leave before the house was flattered by full daylight. Laurie stepped up briskly into the padded interior with her sisters following.

"I do feel rather excited," Clarisse confessed, "though I know I ought to practice detachment. Nuns must be completely detached from personal likes and dislikes. Did Mattie put any plum pie in the basket?"

"Two pieces each," Laurie said.

Thus, amusement at her sister's innocent greed got the start of the journey under way without any tears, save Mattie's, having been shed.

The novelty of the coach ride sufficed to while away the first hours. As the light grew stronger, there was also the pleasure of gazing out at the passing landscape.

Dora, whose delight in nature had never been pronounced, fell into a light doze and snored gently. Fortunately, she looked charming even when she was snoring. Laurie was reassured that her initial determination to provide for Dora by pushing her under Cousin Tarquin's nose had been correct. Once in London, her sister would be provided a fitting backdrop against which her loveliness could appear to best advantage. Then, Tarquin would certainly notice and propose.

Midmorning they stopped at an inn so the girls might refresh themselves. Dora woke as easily as she had slept, her usual good humour unabated. The inn was clean and, having made their toilets, the sisters ordered cider and brought the nuncheon basket out of the carriage. There was a small garden at the side of the inn where the optimistic landlord had put a couple of tables and benches, hoping the sight of customers eating and drinking in the open might entice more to pause and sample his hospitality. the dream had remained a dream since the weather was seldom hot enough for outdoor eating to be possible. In any case his regular patrons preferred to sit in the smoky and inconvenient bar where they could gossip and grumble to their hearts' content.

The arrival of three modestly attired young ladies in a carriage sent him hurrying to wipe benches and set out cushions and, though it was a blow to discover they had brought their own food, he was charmed by Dora's smile into adding fresh rolls and a dish of jam to the feast Mattie had provided.

"We will be in London tonight," Clarisse said, munching on a roll.

"Before tonight, for we've made good time. I heard the coachman saying so," Dora said.

"I wonder if Cousin Tarquin will be at home."

There was a faintly dreamy note in Laurie's voice that made her sisters glance knowingly at each other, but it was gone directly as she added, "I hope he will be a little less stiff and formal in his own home."

"He only recently came back to it though, didn't he?" Dora said. "Perhaps when we know him better he will tell us of all his travels."

"Perhaps." Laurie spoke absently, resolving that if Cousin Tarquin did unbend sufficiently to entertain them, she would steal away and take Clarisse with her so that he might have the encouragement of Dora's wide-eyed attention.

"Oh, do look at that boy," Clarisse exclaimed, pointing beyond the low wall to the road.

A young man had appeared round the bend and drawn rein. Now he was standing in the stirrups and, as they watched, he stepped up cautiously to the saddle and balanced there, his face full of admiration for his own cleverness.

"Heaven's sake! He will break his neck in a moment!" Laurie gasped, but the intrepid rider lowered himself to the saddle again as two other young men galloped round the bend.

"Why did you take off at such a lick?" one of them demanded loudly. "You swore you'd stand in the saddle."

"Which I did. If you'd ridden faster you'd have seen me," the other answered.

He was older than the girls had first imagined, in his early twenties and not his late teens, but his appearance was youthful. His hair curled darkly all over his head, and his eyes were vividly blue as he glanced towards the three sisters.

"You cannot expect to win a wager on your word alone." The second of the newcomers sounded indignant.

"Not on my word alone. The young ladies saw my extraordinary feat."

Laurie rose and pronounced clearly, "We can certainly vouch for the fact that you balanced upon the saddle, sir, though it was not so extraordinary since I understand that performers in circuses do it all the time."

"But not so gracefully," said the young man and favoured her with a smile of such brilliance she found herself smiling back.

"My thanks to you, Miss—"

"St. John." She was not at all sure introductions were either desirable or necessary, but she stepped a little closer to the low wall.

"St. John?" He had dismounted and was staring at her. "Miss Laurentia St. John?"

"Yes, but I fail to see—," she hesitated, puzzled.

"By all that's wonderful, I was on my way to meet you!" He swept off his hat and extended his hand. "Simon St. John, ma'am, at your service."

"He is Cousin Tarquin's brother, Laurie," said Clarisse, jumping up to stand by her sister. "Remember? There were two cousins born."

Until that instant Laurie had forgotten. Now that Tarquin's younger brother had made himself known she could trace a resemblance. Both were tall and dark, though whereas Tarquin's features were harsh his brother had a smoother, more open countenance. His eyes were not blackish-brown but vividly blue, and his mobile mouth was shaped for laughter.

"I do beg your pardon." She strove to collect herself. "I didn't know we were to be met. Cousin Tarquin didn't inform us."

"Tarquin doesn't know," Simon said, putting one hand on top of the wall and vaulting lightly over. "I took it into my head to ride out this direction in the hope of meeting up with you. These are my good friends, Henry Orrin and Percy French." He waved his hand towards the two mounted figures, who swept off their hats and bowed in unison. They were obviously not related but looked curiously similar. Their cravats were similarly and elaborately tied. Their hair was parted on the same side and merged into near identical side whiskers, which were less luxuriant than their owners probably hoped.

"I am Laurie, and this is Dora and Clarisse," Laurie said.

She doubted if the name of her youngest sister had registered at all, since all three of the young men were staring at Dora. Her blue-trimmed straw bonnet framed her face as she sat at the table, a piece of plum pie in her delicate fingers and a welcoming smile on her exquisite lips. Dora always smiled at people as if her whole life had been spent waiting for them to appear. That smile meant absolutely nothing to her, but young men were apt to be struck dumb by its effect.

"Your brother is not coming to meet us himself?" Laurie said.

"Busy with the lawyer fellows. Has been ever since he got back from the Americas," Simon said, his eyes still riveted on Dora. "Did you take nuncheon at the inn? It looks uncommonly good."

"Our housekeeper provided food for us," Dora said, speaking for the first time. The cadences of her voice induced an even more rapt attention in the young men. "The food," she added, "was very good."

"Ambrosia and honey, I'll be bound," said Henry Orrin, dismounting.

"No, just chicken pie and plum tarts and rolls and some pears and seed cake," Dora said.

She was not trying to snub the young man. She simply hadn't noticed the helpless look of instant adoration on his face. Men always looked at Dora in that way. Only Cousin Tarquin had given her the same cool glance he bestowed upon her sisters, but Cousin Tarquin was clearly a cold person. Dora hoped he would improve after he fell in love with Laurie.

"Where's George?" Simon asked. "The coachman? He and Thomas set out together."

"They went to have their food indoors," Clarisse said. As she spoke, the coachman emerged with his companion at his heels.

"Mr. Simon, sir!" His exclamation held a note of alarm. "What are you doing so far along the London road?"

"Coming to meet my cousins and spare you the trouble of driving them," Simon said.

George's expression grew more alarmed still. "Mr. Simon, I promised Mr. Tarquin as how I'd deliver the young ladies without spills or mishaps," he said. "If you've a notion to take over the driving you may put it out of your head."

"In that case I'll race you back to London," Simon replied, unperturbed. "My friends and I will give you a half hour start while we take some refreshment, and then it's the best man wins. Cousins, my compliments."

He swept a very creditable court bow and walked into the inn with a slight swagger. His two friends, both gazing at Dora, raised their voices for the services of an ostler and followed.

"I do beg that you will put any notion of racing out of your head," Laurie said to the coachman anxiously.

"Don't fret, ma'am." George had a most reassuring manner. "I've no intention of racing anywhere and well he knows it. It was only Mr. Simon's bit of funning, miss."

Hoping he was right, Laurie gathered up the remains of the nuncheon and shepherded her sisters back into the carriage.

"Simon is not in the least like his brother, is he?"

Clarisse chattered.

"I certainly cannot imagine Cousin Tarquin doing circus tricks in the middle of the public highway," said Laurie dryly.

She spoke the more severely because there had been something irrepressibly attractive about the handsome young man. He was all charm and lightness where his elder brother was dour. He was the kind of young man to whom Dora might finally lose her heart, and Dora must be steered towards marriage with Tarquin.

Almost an hour passed before the three young gentlemen caught up with them. From their whooping and waving, Laurie surmised they had drunk something stronger than cider at the inn. They were not exactly foxed but perilously near it. She was relieved beyond measure when the increasing traffic forced them to drop back.

She had always pictured London as a great, walled city, thick with spires and bright with bells, but there was no actual instant when she was able to say to herself that they had entered the capital. They drove first through a series of villages, until those became one long village and the coach was rattling over cobbles. Through the window she could see houses and shops and hurrying people and hear the babble of voices mingled with the barking dogs and rumbling coaches. Then, the cobbles gave way to a smooth paved surface, and the crowds thinned out as the buildings fell back to form a series of squares. She glimpsed trees trapped behind railings and the gleam of a lake, and a few moments later they rattled into a wide yard where the coach stopped.

The door was opened by the coachman, who had clambered down and now stood beaming, as if he had brought them unscathed through unimaginable dangers.

"If you will kindly step round to the front door," he said, "your luggage will be taken up."

An archway led into the square with its facades of handsome houses and wide pavement planted with cherry trees. The trees looked self-conscious in their isolation, but at least there were trees. Laurie's spirits rose as she went up the front steps to the doorway with a delicate fanlight above it.

The arrival of the carriage had evidently been noted. As she raised her hand to the bell push, the door was opened from within. A footman, looking splendid in his livery of dark blue and silver, bowed and stood aside.

A narrow lobby gave way to a wider hall, with a staircase curving upward to the left and doorways to left and right. It needed only one glance round the hall for Laurie to realise that her cousin had not exaggerated his means. The walls were hung with a silk paper in a fine gold and white stripe, and the thin rugs on the polished floor were Chinese. A carved table held several ornaments of jade and onyx, and the drapes at the tall windows were made of silk. There would be no leaking roofs or tumbledown barns in this house.

A maidservant in a crisply frilled apron appeared and bobbed a curtsey. "If you'll follow me, Miss St. John?" She spoke to Laurie but included the others in her glance.

The staircase ascended to a closed gallery which was carpeted and lined with doors. Walking along it, Laurie was again conscious of the pristine condition of everything, and the luxury of the patterned red and gold carpet under her feet. The doors were all painted white, their panels picked out in gold, and light slanted down from skylights high above them. The maidservant opened a door near the end of the gallery and stood back politely as they entered.

This chamber was a drawing room, curtained in blue and cream and tastefully furnished. If a speck of dust ever dared to show itself here, it would be instantly annihilated, Laurie was certain of that. Her next thought was the alarming suspicion that she might have picked up a little dirt on the sole of her shoe and was desecrating the cream rug. She forgot both considerations as a slim, dark woman—with Tarquin's features cast in a feminine mould—spoke from the chaise longue where she was reclining.

"I do hope your journey was not too terribly fatiguing?"

The voice had only the barest trace of a French accent. Its tone conveyed boredom rather than any pressing desire to have an answer to the question, and the hand the lady extended was limp and cool.

"Very comfortable, thank you—Aunt Marie?" Laurie wondered if she was expected to shake the hand or kiss it. She touched it briefly with her own gloved fingers and dropped a curtsey.

"Carriage rides can be so dreadfully tedious," the other said. Her eyes, sharper than her voice and manner, roved from one face to the next. "You must be Laurentia?"

"I'm called Laurie, ma'am."

Her aunt looked as if that were a pity, but merely nodded.

"I'm Clarisse and this is Dora," Clarisse said in the high voice that meant she was nervous and had resolved not to betray it.

"Also shortened?" Aunt Marie enquired.

"Dora is really Theodora, and sometimes people call me Clary. Are we to call you Aunt?"

"Were we in my beloved France, then Tante would be appropriate, but since we are in England Aunt will suffice," the other said. "I usually take my nap at this hour of the afternoon, but since your arrival was expected—"

"We could have timed it more conveniently had we known," Laurie said, "but Cousin Tarquin gave the instructions for departure to the coachman."

She could feel her temper beginning to rise and held it back with an effort. Aunt Marie might not be particularly welcoming, but it would be foolish to make an enemy of Dora's future mother-in-law.

"None of you is like your father in looks," Aunt Marie said. It was impossible to tell from her tone if she was pleased about that or not.

"I believe I am the most like, Aunt," Laurie said, determined to be pleasant. "Dora is like Mama, though I don't recall her, of course, and Clarisse is—she is simply Clarisse."

"I cannot recollect my late husband ever mentioning there being red hair in the family," Aunt Marie pursued. "However, there are throwbacks, I believe. I will have Jane show you to your rooms. Fortunately, there are several guest rooms so you will not be cramped. Are those the only garments you have with you?"

"No indeed, Aunt," Laurie said coldly. "We brought a deal of luggage."

"We will see about your wardrobes later." Aunt Marie raised a languid hand. "I am glad you are not wearing black. I cannot abide black."

The maidservant had entered again and was holding open the door. Laurie managed to smile as she curtsied, but it demanded an effort. For two pins she would have sat down and burst into tears, but as the eldest it behooved her to retain her self-possession. Nevertheless, her cheekbones were dyed an indignant scarlet as she followed the little maidservant along the gallery and up a second flight of stairs to a corridor that branched left and right. Their rooms were in the right-hand wing, and she was forced to admit that they compared very favourably with what she had already seen of the rest of the house. Each room was a decent size, furnished in fine taste and hung with muslin and silk of pastel shades, which gave the rooms a light and charming air. The maid vanished, murmuring something about hot water. Her departure was the signal for the sisters to clamour into what was the largest of the rooms where their baggage had already been deposited.

"I usually take my nap at this hour," Clarisse imitated in an unflattering tone, "but since you've been so inconsiderate as to descend upon me—she doesn't want us here at all. She hasn't the faintest desire to launch any of us into Society."

"It is probably just her style," said Dora. "She is French."

"She hasn't any manners," Clarisse sniffed. "Why did we have to come, Laurie? Cousin Tarquin couldn't have forced us to obey him if we'd stood firm, could he?"

"It is very kind of him to think about our futures at all," Laurie said firmly. She had mastered her temper and spoke reproachfully. "This is a very grand house, and she is unused to the company of young girls. We must give her time to adapt to us."

The thought sprung to mind that they would be the ones doing the adapting, but Laurie pushed it uneasily aside.

4

BY THE TIME they had washed off the dust of the journey and combed their hair, all three of the girls felt better able to face whatever the evening might bring. They had changed their travelling dresses for lighter evening wear, and when a gong sounded from below, they obeyed its summons with alacrity.

The maidservant, Jane, was on the staircase to direct them to the dining room. She was the only person who had given them a smile since they entered the house. Laurie smiled back as she led her sisters across the hall to the double doors being opened by the footman.

The dining room was as handsomely appointed as the rest of the house. There were silver, crystal, and low copper bowls filled with pinks against a background of Sheraton chairs and table and a beautifully woven pair of screens in the Florentine manner.

Their aunt was already seated. It was Tarquin who came forward to greet them. This formal setting suited his dark elegance, and his greeting was more cordial than his mother's had been.

"Did you have a good journey? We are dining early tonight as I suspect you feel the need for sustenance. Travelling always gives me an appetite. Are your rooms to your liking?"

"Very much so." Laurie spoke for all of them. "We are unaccustomed to so much space."

"It will be pleasant to have the house full again. I understand you have met Simon?"

They were seating themselves and it was Clarisse who answered incautiously, "Standing up in the saddle just as they do in the circus. It looked exceedingly clever."

"And exceedingly dangerous!" Aunt Marie had paled. "Tarquin, you must speak to him at once."

"I will do so." Tarquin sounded rather grim.

"He knows how much such behaviour upsets me."

Laurie remembered that her uncle had been killed in a riding accident and sent a warning frown down the table to her sister, who realised she had been tactless and clapped a hand over her mouth. Fortunately, their first course was being served by two white-gloved footmen under the direction of an extremely imposing butler, and that distracted from Clarisse's *faux pas*.

"Will Cousin Simon be joining us?" Laurie enquired.

"My brother has numerous engagements," Tarquin began but was interrupted by the banging of the front door. His sibling strode into the dining room just in time to catch the end of that sentence.

"But none that would keep me from the company of my fair cousins," he said. "Why didn't we know they were a trio of beauties?"

He was slighter in frame than his elder brother. His hair was curlier also, and his complexion fair. Laurie thought again of the contrast between darkness and light which they embodied.

"We have just learned of your dangerous antics to impress this bevy of fair cousins," said Tarquin dryly. "Must you always seek the limelight?"

"Only when I have an audience," Simon answered, bending to kiss his mother's cheek.

Laurie noticed that her aunt's rather hard face had softened perceptibly and there was a quirk at the corners of Tarquin's mouth. Meanwhile, Clarisse stared at the young man with the beginnings of hero worship in her gaze, but Dora merely sipped her soup placidly. Laurie breathed a little sigh of relief. It would not do for Dora to fall in love with the wrong brother. That Dora hadn't yet shown a sign of falling in love with anybody didn't enter the elder sister's head.

"If you went to meet our cousins, why did you not escort them to the house?" Tarquin was enquiring.

"Got waylaid by a couple of dunning scoundrels," Simon said.

"Meaning you are in debt again?" Tarquin flashed his brother a sharp look.

"Meaning I prefer to talk about more congenial subjects," said Simon.

"How much?" Tarquin insisted.

"Fifty guineas, my dear fellow. A mere bagatelle. I will settle the matter over the next few days."

"See that you do," said Tarquin coldly as Aunt Marie rushed into the breach.

"We will have to see about dresses for Laurentia and Dora, if they are to be launched in a suitable manner."

"Like ships," Clarisse said and giggled when Simon chuckled.

"I have already told Cousin Tarquin that I have no intention of imposing on his generosity or his good nature," Laurie hastened to say.

"It is not a matter of either," said Aunt Marie, "but a matter of what is fitting for my husband's nieces."

Laurie wondered what had prompted such concern when throughout their childhood their uncle and aunt had failed to recognise their existence. Apart from a brief note of sympathy, they had similarly ignored the death of Laurence St. John. Argument, however, would have been both useless and ill bred. There was also the added consideration of Dora, who would certainly create a stir when she emerged properly wardrobed into Society and thus force Tarquin to look at her with more attention. For Dora's sake Laurie must keep a still tongue in her head.

"What accomplishments have you?" her aunt was now enquiring. "Both of you have studied the pianoforte?"

"With Miss Browne, our governess," Laurie said. "We all play and sing a little."

"And dancing classes? There were dancing classes?"

With Miss Browne thumping the pianoforte and Mattie dragged in to partner Clarisse, thought Laurie with an inward grin. Aloud she said, "Yes indeed, Aunt."

"I like cooking too," Clarisse put in. "I love making up dishes for people to try."

Her remark was greeted with raised eyebrows. "As it will be at least a year before you will be making your debut in polite society, my dear, we must hope to instill more ladylike talents in you by then."

The meal wore on, interspersed with occasional snippets of conversation between mother and sons. Laurie listened to the nuances of the voices and observed the play of varying expressions over the three faces, then came to the conclusion that Simon was his mother's favourite but Tarquin commanded her respect. Between the brothers she sensed an affection tinged on the elder's part with exasperation and, on the younger's, with the desire to tease.

"Now we shall have coffee and a little music," Aunt Marie said at length. "Laurentia, will you not begin?"

The music room opened out of the dining room and contained a handsome pianoforte, as well as two Spanish guitars on the wall and a small harp in the corner. Laurie seated herself obediently on the piano stool and wondered who played the latter.

While coffee was served and handed round by the footman, she played a short selection of traditional tunes which required little concentration. Unlike Dora, who had a real gift she was too lazy to develop, Laurie was only an adequate musician. Nonetheless, her performance called forth approving applause.

"Very pleasant, my dear," said her aunt. "Now come and drink your coffee while Dora entertains us."

Dora rose with her usual grace to take her place on the piano stool. The candelabra above the instrument cast a golden light over her curls, and her cheeks were faintly flushed. She played by ear, her white fingers caressing the keys, her head bent slightly as if she sought to lose herself in the music.

Laurie sipped her excellent coffee and stole a glance at Tarquin, who had seated himself a little distance from the rest and was listening intently. His dark head inclined towards Dora, and his eyes fixed on her with what was clearly great admiration.

So far so good, Laurie thought, without asking herself why she didn't feel better pleased about it. What she did feel was a sense of depression which she attributed to the long coach drive and the unfamiliar surroundings.

"That was exquisite, Cousin Dora," said Tarquin as the melody trailed into silence. "I don't believe I know the piece."

"I made it up. I usually do make up my own music."

"But you can read other people's works?"

"Not as well as Laurie," Dora answered frankly.

"There is a Mozart sonata which I have never heard played in the way it ought to be played." He had risen and moved towards her to open a small chest in which sheet music was kept. "I know you have had an exhausting day, but would you oblige me by trying it?"

"I have an appointment," said Simon with somewhat ungallant haste. "Would you excuse me?"

"It would be so agreeable if you could spend just one evening at home," Aunt Marie complained.

"My dearest mama, you should be happy that your son is so popular," he chided. "When my duties permit, I hope you will not grudge me the pleasure of an hour or two with my friends."

"From what I've observed, your duties seem to be remarkably elastic," Tarquin commented dryly.

"But onerous. Cousins, welcome again. I trust I'll have the delight of your company very soon." He waved his hand and was gone, his footsteps light in the passage.

Dora had meanwhile begun to play the sonata, stumblingly at first, then with more confidence. It was astonishing how, with little or no practice, she could manage to find the heart of the music and render it with feeling.

"Would you think me very rude if I begged to be excused?" Laurie heard herself saying.

"You have a headache?" Her aunt gave her a concerned look.

"The beginnings of one," Laurie answered, realising that to be actually true. "I am not used to travelling, ma'am."

"By all means. I'll have Jane bring you a tisane. I find Jane's tisanes invaluable for my own occasional megrims," her aunt said, more cordially than she had yet spoken.

"I haven't got a headache," Clarisse said hastily, seeing her aunt's gaze drift in her direction. "I shall play something for you if you like."

"I think we have been sufficiently entertained this evening," Aunt Marie said. "Your musical ability will not be called upon until next year."

"Though I hope we shall hear you play for us before then many times," Tarquin said with a kindliness in his tone which made Laurie feel suddenly better. "Mama, you must excuse me too. I also have an engagement. Cousin Dora, you must make regular time for practice. A gift like yours ought not to be neglected."

He bowed and then was gone, striding out with a tread noticeably heavier than his brother's.

"Perhaps we had all better say good night?" It was clear from the look on Aunt Marie's face that she considered the company of her nieces poor exchange for the absence of her sons.

The girls bade her good night and went upstairs, Clarisse turning to make a face at the closed panels of the door.

"Clary!" scolded Dora.

"I hope she saw me," said Clarisse unrepentantly. "Her eyes can probably bore through doors like gimlets. She is quite the most impossible aunt one could imagine. I am certain she regards us as a very great imposition and doesn't want to launch any of us into any kind of society."

Laurie was inclined to agree with her but felt it incumbent to add her chiding to Dora's. "Fine talk from a prospective nun, I must say! What happened to gratitude and charity?"

"Why should we be grateful to leave our home and spend the year here?" Clarisse demanded. "And I don't feel charitable. She looks down her nose at us as if we were orphans."

"We are," Dora reminded her.

"Abandoned orphans," Clarisse said and emphasised her feelings by slamming her bedroom door.

"She is feeling homesick," said Dora. "I rather like this house, as a matter of fact. It is pleasant to have one's meal served so elegantly and the pianoforte has a beautiful tone. I am resolved to practise regularly."

"Cousin Tarquin greatly admired your playing," Laurie said warmly.

"Oh, he clearly has an educated taste in music," said Dora before passing into her own room.

Marriage would fit Dora like a glove, Laurie thought, gazing after her sister. She would develop into a charming and accomplished hostess and, with her good nature, there was no risk of her quarrelling with her mother-in-law. Tarquin was already attracted. A few more sonatas and he would be naming the day.

At the moment, however, the prospect of entering her new pastel-shaded bedroom and lying awake for hours did not appeal to Laurie. She took a cloak from the peg where someone, probably Jane, had hung it and went down the staircase again. The front door was closed, and she would probably be seen crossing the hall. A short passage behind the stairs brought her to an unlocked side door which opened into the stableyard. There were gardens beyond the coach house and an archway, but she turned instead into the street.

The long evenings of summer had taken on the first chill of autumn, and the twilight drained colour from the neatly planted cherry trees. Here and there in the quiet square light glowed from still uncurtained windows, and the sun was a curve of orange red above the rooftops. Walking had always been one of her particular pleasures. Back home, she often took a brisk turn in the village or wandered farther afield where the houses gave way to meadow and grove.

At first this elegant square seemed to offer little in the way of a stroll, but a few minutes' walk brought her to a narrow alley between the houses and the iron railings of a park beyond. A park was as close to real countryside as she was likely to get in London, so she took that direction. The hard pavements were making her feet ache, and she anticipated with pleasure the softness of grass where she could ramble and forget her depression.

The gates were open. She passed through into the ordered wilderness of lawn and bush and gravel pathways which led off in various directions and were bordered by elms. It was obviously an extensive park, and Laurie's spirits lifted as the scent of night-blooming verbena drifted toward her nostrils.

She was not, it seemed, the only person who enjoyed a twilight stroll. There were one or two couples walking together, the females of the pairs linking arms with their taller companions. Several young ladies passed by chattering in an accent she guessed was Cockney. There were benches at intervals, and she stepped aside to rest on one for a moment or two. Her headache had ceased to threaten, and, in the fresh air, the depression that had cast her down was abating.

"Good evening, ma'am."

The voice belonged to a gentleman who wore an immensely large ruby on the hand he held out to her. His face was in shadow from the brim of his tall hat, but she was conscious that he was attempting to get a closer look at her.

Company was the last thing Laurie wanted. She made a polite murmur and turned her head away. The next moment, to her astonished horror, the stranger had seized her arm and jerked her to her feet.

"Hoity-toity, aren't we?" his voice said in her ear.

In that second Laurie became aware that this was not the countryside where greetings were exchanged by passing strangers without any invasion of privacy. The place where she stood contained only herself and a large, intimidating man whom she could no longer regard as a gentleman, and he had clearly mistaken her for someone else. Fright held her rigid for an instant. Then she ducked her head and sank her teeth into the beringed hand.

Her assailant let out a distinctly ungentlemanly oath and loosed his hold. Laurie didn't wait to find out if her bite had drawn blood. She wrenched herself free and ran, as fast as her narrow skirts would allow, back towards the main gate, but the path most unfairly twisted in the wrong direction and brought her to a low stone wall with a side street beyond.

She had no idea if she was being pursued or not. Fortunately, her childhood had not been devoid of trees to climb. She shinned over the modest parapet, hearing the seam of her skirt rip as she landed on the other side. She reasoned that if she followed the wall to where the iron railings began she would find the alley that led back into the square.

She started to run, her heartbeats drumming in her ears, but they were not heartbeats at all. They were the hooves of a horse bearing down on her. She ran faster, desperately trying to swerve, but the pursuer was gaining and her breath was spent. She reeled back against the wall and stood gasping for air, as the rider drew rein and dismounted.

"Cousin Laurie, what the devil are you doing out here?"

She recognised the voice even in the midst of her panic. Tarquin was staring at her in astonishment which was visible despite the fading light.

"I was—taking a stroll," she replied lamely, biting back a sudden desire to cast herself into his arms and burst into humiliating tears.

"By yourself? At night?" He sounded as if she had just broken the law.

"I thought someone was following me," she said, suspecting that her account of having been attacked would meet with scant sympathy.

"I'm surprised you have not been accosted," he returned. "What was my mother thinking to let you wander out alone?"

"Your mother knows nothing about it," Laurie said earnestly, "and I do beg that you will not inform her. I frequently take a stroll about the neighbourhood at home."

"This is London," he interrupted, "where ladies do not stroll unaccompanied even during the daylight hours. You must surely have been aware of that?"

"It slipped my mind."

"And your dress is torn!" He indicated her white-stockinged leg visible through the long rent in her skirt.

"I climbed over the wall."

"Instead of going through the gate?" he asked, as if he were beginning to think her wildly eccentric.

"The paths," she said vaguely, "were confusing."

"I'll take you home." He bent down without warning, picked her up, and sat her on the horse.

"I can walk," she began to protest, but was curtly interrupted.

"You had best sit still and hold on. I don't use a side saddle."

There was nothing for it but to grit her teeth and hold on as he suggested. If she'd had the sense to blurt out the truth the moment she saw him, she wouldn't have given him the impression that she was completely lacking in common sense. Then, however, he might have insisted on finding her assailant and involving them both in a public uproar. As no real harm had been done, she decided she had been wiser to remain quiet. That London parks were dangerous after dark was a fact she had heard before without taking much notice. She would not be so unmindful again.

Meanwhile, Tarquin had looped the reins over his arm and was leading the horse towards home.

"I take it that you slipped away through the side door," he commented. "By now my mother has probably had a satisfying attack of hysteria."

"Everybody thinks me in my room," she confessed. "I came out for a walk on impulse."

"Then with a little luck we can get you back into your room without alerting the entire household. I do trust you will curb your impulses in future, Cousin."

"I am not accustomed to formality," she retorted.

"In the country that doesn't matter, but here in the city polite society thrives on custom and ritual."

"How exceedingly dull."

Her cousin had turned away, and she was not sure if she imagined a stifled laugh. They had gone through the alley and were approaching the house. As they went round to the courtyard at the side she felt obliged to thank him for his help.

"I do realise, Cousin Tarquin, that it was somewhat unconventional of me to take a stroll. I will avoid such imprudence in future."

"See that you do." He swung her to the cobbles and held her lightly for a moment, his face all angles and planes in the moonlight.

"Dora played beautifully, don't you agree?" she said quickly before the silence between them could become embarrassing.

"Exquisitely," he nodded, releasing her. "I shall insist that she practises regularly in future. I hope you will add your voice to mine."

"Even if she played badly she would still look extremely pretty doing it."

"Extremely pretty," he said. "She has a certain way of

turning her head that is most delightful. She is a charming girl altogether."

"Goodnight again, Cousin, and thank you."

Laurie pulled her cloak about her torn dress and stepped towards the door, which yielded to her touch. She glanced back and saw him remount and ride out into the square. She gained her room without meeting anyone and hastily removed her garments. The quilt had been folded back and the candles trimmed and lit. From the adjoining chambers came no sound.

Tarquin certainly admired Dora, Laurie reflected, reaching for the brush to begin her obligatory hundred strokes. When he saw Dora admired by other gentlemen, his feelings would grow even stronger. It was all going to turn out as Laurie had planned. There could be no reason save homesickness for the tears in her eyes.

= 5 =

"IF I HAVE to stand here for one more fitting, I'm certain my legs will drop off entirely." Laurie cast herself into the armchair with a lack of grace her aunt would have deplored. Every moment of the three weeks they had spent in London had been occupied with preparations for the social debuts of herself and Dora. She'd scarcely had time to catch her breath.

Whatever Aunt Marie's private opinion of her nieces, she was evidently determined to launch them in style. An army of milliners, seamstresses, hosiers, hairdressers, shoemakers, and florists had processed through the house, all of them bringing skills and wares designed to transform two country cousins into social butterflies. She and Dora had been measured, fitted, refitted, poked with whalebone stays, tortured with curling irons, and constantly nagged by their aunt, who make it her business to find out every little thing they were doing and immediately disapprove.

Laurie's plain-spoken ways were stigmatised as gauche. Her hair, which she refused to cut, was pronounced unfortunate. Her habit of reading books heavier than novels had been declared a grievous fault.

"You play and sing very sweetly," Aunt Marie admitted graciously, "and you have a lively manner. But, pray, never allow any gentlemen to guess that you enjoy Shakespeare in the original, or that you find dancing tedious."

Dora had fared rather better. She had been found wanting only in a certain lack of energy. However, her musical talent, her very pretty soprano voice, her nimble dancing, and her complete disinterest in culture had all been praised.

None of the clothes they had brought with them were considered suitable for anything grander than a quiet evening at home. From the list of social engagements piling up in the silver invitations tray, it appeared that evenings at home were destined to be rare.

Laurie worried about the cost of all the frills and furbelows which hung in the wardrobes and bulged out of the drawers, but to talk about money was, Aunt Marie assured her, in very bad taste.

"I am so thankful that I am not coming out," said Clarisse from the window seat where she was perched. "It will be a great waste of time for me even next year, if Aunt insists, since I intend to renounce the world anyway."

"How can you possibly renounce something you know nothing about?" Laurie asked sensibly.

"I know quite sufficient, thank you. Vanity of vanities is a most sensible quotation in my opinion."

"I don't suppose whoever wrote that had the opportunity of being presented at Court," Dora mused. "It will be rather interesting to see the royal family. Only think, Queen Charlotte has had fifteen children."

"No wonder the poor king has run mad," remarked Clarisse.

"It will be the Prince Regent to whom we make our curtseys," Dora reminded. "He is one of the most fashionable gentlemen in Europe."

"I heard he was overweight," said Clarisse.

"As you will be if you don't stop chewing," said Laurie. "It is less than two hours since luncheon, and here you are eating chocolate again."

"I have hollow legs."

Her elder sisters stared at her in consternation.

"Good heavens, Clary, where in the world did you pick up such an inelegant expression?" Laurie demanded.

"Cousin Simon said that I had," Clarisse informed them as she bit into another chocolate.

Dora giggled, but Laurie frowned. Their cousin Simon was frequently at home, his duties at Court being apparently of the lightest. Though he went out almost every evening, he generally contrived to spend part of the day with the girls, teasing and flirting in a manner very different from that of his older brother. Having seen his cousins established, Tarquin took no notice of them beyond a polite greeting when they met. He too was usually absent at night, and when he was at home he devoted himself to Dora with an enthusiasm that Laurie told herself was very pleasing.

"Simon uses some very coarse expressions," Laurie scolded. "He fancies himself as a nonpareil, but he is actually rather foolish and immature."

"And very charming," Dora observed. "I believe that if he found the right girl he would settle down."

Laurie threw her an apprehensive look. Dora mustn't develop a *tendresse* for the feckless Simon now. It would spoil all the plans that Laurie had made. Besides, Simon was too lightweight for Dora.

"He has not the character of his brother," said Laurie firmly. "There are depths to Tarquin."

Instead of arguing, Dora looked pleased. "Cousin Tarquin has a very interesting character," she said. "Clarisse and I have both remarked it."

They were the first words of praise that Laurie had ever heard her bestow on their elder cousin. Perhaps, Dora was beginning to appreciate his more sober and adult personality.

"Certainly he will make some fortunate young lady an excellent husband," Laurie added. "And whoever weds him will be mistress of Gables, too."

"It seems years since we were at home," said Clarisse wistfully. "I do miss it so."

Laurie felt a pang of sympathy. Poor Clarisse had been largely overlooked in the fuss about her sisters' coming-out. So far, the promised sight-seeing trips hadn't materialised. Apart from stiffly correct and formal carriage rides with Aunt Marie, they had none of them been anywhere.

"You have reminded me that I must write to Mattie," she said abruptly. "I will do it at once before I forget."

When Laurie had quitted the room, the younger girls looked at each other.

"Do you think she is beginning to admire him?" Dora asked.

"It is more to the point whether or not Cousin Tarquin is beginning to admire her. He is so seldom at home, and when he is he hangs about you."

"Only because he likes music."

"But you ought not to encourage it. Think how dreadful it would be if he admired you more than Laurie."

"I do try to sing his praises to her when opportunity arises," Dora excused herself. "But one never knows what Laurie is thinking."

At that instant Laurie would have been hard put to tell what she was thinking herself. She had retreated to the study and was trying to compose a letter to Mattie that would reassure her as to their well-being without making the housekeeper feel they had ceased to miss her.

> My Dear Mattie,
> I would have written before, but the days here are filled up with preparations for Dora's and my coming-out. We have scarcely a moment left to blink. The house is very elegant and in a secluded square, and Aunt Marie has spared no pains to turn us into young society ladies. We are to be presented at Court at the beginning of next month after which we may accept invitations to balls and other events.
> Let me tell you about the dresses that have been decided upon for our coming-out ball. For

the actual presentation we shall both wear the regulation white and silver with ostrich plumes, but after that colours are permitted. Aunt Marie has agreed that under the circumstances, we are justified in leaving off mourning. I believe that Papa would have approved since he always had a horror of black. For the actual ball Dora will wear a beautiful gown of pale blue silk embroidered with clusters of silver leaves. The neckline and the hem have a deep, pleated ruche trimmed with tiny bows, and she has a very pretty ornament of silver leaves to decorate her hair. I am convinced that all the gentlemen will fall in love with her. My own dress is of similar mode, but rose pink with an overall pattern of gold daisies in silk and a spray of gold daisies for my hair. So I too hope not to be a wall-flower. Those are not the only new gowns we have. It would take far too long to describe everything to you. You must content yourself with the knowledge that we have never been so elegant in our lives.

I trust you are keeping well and are not too inconvenienced by the workmen who will have descended upon Gables. I hope the renovations they make are not too radical, since the dear old place has a character of its own that ought to be preserved. I have no idea what plans have been made for after the winter season. I believe that Cousin Tarquin will not do anything until our social season is over. I doubt if he intends to live permanently in the country, but he may spend long periods there. That is only speculation since the matter has not been discussed.

Both Cousin Tarquin and Cousin Simon will escort us to the Presentation. They live at home but are frequently at their clubs and in Simon's case at Court. He is an amusing and likable young man, less reserved than his brother. I cannot understand how the latter ever got a reputation for being wild. For a man not yet thirty he is as grave as forty.

    I will draw to a close now, my dear Mattie. Dora and Clarisse both send love and will write themselves before very long.
        Your affectionate friend,
            Laurie St. John.

She was sanding the paper and reaching for the waxen seal when a cough at the door heralded Tarquin's entrance.

"Are you busy, Cousin Laurie?" He spoke with his usual chilly politeness. The evening when she had run away in the park had never been referred to again.

"I was writing to Mattie," Laurie told him. "I have just concluded without saying half of what I intended to say when I began."

"Letters are poor substitutes for conversations," he nodded. "Do you miss Mattie? She has been more than a servant to you all your life."

"I miss everything," Laurie said, and was horrified to feel her lip quivering. "City life is very confining when one is a female."

"Would you like to ride with me? I am taking Jasper for some exercise on the heath, and Rainbow would benefit from some too."

She had been weary, but the prospect of a canter in the fresh air brought the energy surging back.

"If you can give me five minutes? I will seal this and ask Jane to post it, then put on my habit."

"I'll instruct Thomas to put a lady's saddle on Rainbow," he said.

The severe lines of the grey riding habit suited her slender figure. She adjusted the tricorne hat on her neatly pinned hair and hurried down to the yard, where she found her cousin already mounted. Only when she herself was perched on Rainbow and they were trotting across the square with the groom riding behind did she remember that she had not informed her sisters she was going out.

"I told Dora and Clarisse that we were off for a gallop, so nobody will be seeking you," said Tarquin.

"I hope they were not hurt at being excluded. It is a long time since they rode."

"They are neither of them in any hurry to go riding now either," he assured her. "Dora announced her intention of taking a nap, and Clarisse gave us leave not to hurry back."

In that case, Laurie decided with relief, she could enjoy herself with a clear conscience. Though it would have accorded better with her plans if he had invited Dora to ride, there was no denying that Dora was not a horsewoman. She looked charming in the saddle, but if her mount dared to canter she clung to the reins and begged to go home.

The heath was the nearest thing to countryside she had seen since her adventure in the park. It stretched in all directions in billows and valleys of fading green, with thorn bushes and wild flowers and trees to add character to the landscape. Here and there smoke rose up from the chimneys of cottages buried deep amid the bracken.

"Squatters," Tarquin said, noting her look. "There is an old law giving anyone who can build a house with a roof within twenty-four hours the right to remain. People still take advantage of it occasionally."

"Is the heath as dangerous as the park?" she asked.

"Not where we are riding. Were you anticipating an attack by footpads? Both William and I are well armed, I promise you."

"That is a sport that has always interested me," she said impulsively.

"Robbing people?"

"No, shooting. Not people, merely targets. Papa taught me how to cock, aim, and fire and even spoke of getting me a lady's pistol, but he never did."

Her father, she thought, had been a great one for promising, but somehow or other the promises never materialised.

"We must have a contest sometime," her cousin said, looking amused. "For now we will content ourselves with a gallop. Do you see that clump of trees over there? I will give you a start—"

"I don't require one," she interrupted, nettled by his condescension.

"As you please." He gave her a brisk nod. "In that event, we're off!"

Within a couple of minutes Laurie realised that she had needed the start after all. Jasper was a faster and more powerful horse than the more docile Rainbow, and it was some time since she had been in the saddle. Lowering her head, she gripped the reins and urged the horse on, wishing she had the advantage of riding astride so she could have used her knees to increase the pace. The trees which had seemed very close were farther off than she had thought, and Jasper was well ahead.

Nevertheless, the ride was exhilarating. The wind blew strands of hair about her temples and whipped colour into her cheeks. When she finally drew rein, her eyes were sparkling.

"That was splendid, and I concede victory," she informed her cousin, who had dismounted and come over to assist her to the ground.

"You ought to have accepted that start, but you ride well. Some girls look like sacks of flour on horseback. You look like Diana."

"Who went about with a pack of dogs hunting down men," Laurie said wryly.

"Only when she was in a bad humour. Come, I want to introduce you to some friends of mine."

William had come forward to hold the horses, and Tarquin took Laurie's arm and led her along a path that twisted between the trees. The path dipped down into a hollow and she saw brightly painted caravans and a huddle of children and barking dogs.

"Gypsies?" She stopped dead, looking up into his face.

"You have friends among the Gypsies?"

"Romanies," he corrected. "The Bohannas are pure Romany, not tinker. They remind me of some of the native Indian tribes I saw when I was in the Americas. They too live according to ancient tradition and scorn conformity. Come."

He was urging her down into the hollow. Closer to, she could smell the mingled odours of babies, animals, cooking, and an indefinable, subtle scent that had no physical cause but was, she decided, the scent of strangeness. One or two of the dogs ran up barking, but a man of about Tarquin's age emerged from one of the gaily painted caravans and called them to heel before striding up to Tarquin with hands outstretched and a smile on his swarthy face.

"Tarquin St. John, it is too long since you visited us."

"I brought my cousin, Miss Laurie," Tarquin said, gripping the other's hands briefly. "I would like you to meet Ianto, Cousin. Ianto Bohanna is a good friend of mine. He saved my life once, but will be angry if I make much of it. Are all well?"

"Well enough." The man called Ianto had a slight singsong accent which made even the commonplace remark musical. "Mama Sarah will be glad to see you. She will not be surprised. She said yesterday she felt you would be visiting soon."

"Since I usually try to get over once in every month it didn't require any great power of divination to forecast that."

"Your cousin makes mock, Miss Laurie," Ianto said without rancour. "My grandmother has the sight, though."

"I never had my fortune told," Laurie said.

"She will tell yours, though I could do that myself after one glance at your face."

He gave her a flattering look from long-lashed black eyes.

"My cousin is impervious to your charms, my friend,"

Tarquin said laughing. "She is country bred and has no romantic notions about Gypsies."

They had reached the largest of the caravans where wooden steps led up to a curtained arch. The curtain was looped back, and Laurie had a view of a crowded, cramped, but very neat and clean interior. Her attention was riveted almost immediately, however, by the woman who sat on the steps. She was tall and angular with immense gold hoops in her ears and traces of great beauty in her brown face. Her white-streaked black hair hung in heavy braids, and her arms were decorated with gold bangles that jangled when she moved.

"Mama Sarah, may I present my cousin, Miss Laurentia St. John?" Tarquin sounded respectful. Laurie was not surprised by that as she met the piercing black gaze of the eyes turned to look at her. There were some people who, whatever their circumstances, had about them the aura of power, and this woman was one such.

In contrast to her years, her voice was light, almost girlish. "You have silver in your eyes, Laurie St. John," she said.

"And will cross your palm with some," Tarquin said, taking coins out and handing them to Laurie.

Mama Sarah accepted them as tribute and took both Laurie's hands in a brisk, businesslike way like that of a physician.

"Ianto, take Tarquin away to drink some ale," she commanded. "A woman is entitled to keep her future to herself."

"I don't really believe in such things," Laurie said, feeling embarrassed as the two men moved away and the old woman continued to study her palms.

"Belief makes no matter," Mama Sarah said. "The lines on your left hand show the way your life could go and the lines on your right hand show what use you've made of your gifts. You are young yet, so there's time for the lines to change in the way you choose. I can see loving in your hand, but not enough for yourself. Learn to be more selfish."

"Nobody ever told me to do that before," Laurie said in surprise.

"If you don't love and care for yourself, you can't love and care fully for anyone else," Mama Sarah said. "You have a meddlesome nature, trying to arrange other lives into the pattern you want to see, but you must learn to let people make their own patterns."

"What about my future?" Laurie began to feel a trifle impatient with what sounded like a moral lecture.

"You'll travel in a strange land," Mama Sarah said, "with the man of your heart if you choose right, or you'll wither down into old age if you choose wrong. Destiny's of our own choosing. You have two sisters."

"Tarquin told you," Laurie accused.

"Tarquin said nothing. One of your sisters is destined to become famous. The other will live a country life. There's a hanging here, a topping plain as plain. You have an enemy, a man with a ruby on his hand."

"I don't want to hear any more," Laurie said, pulling her hands away, her face paling slightly. "I told you that I don't believe in such things."

"Ah, but you're educated," Mama Sarah said, "and the educated never had much sense. I wish you joy, girl, and your heart's desire, but that's for you to reach out and take."

Laurie straightened up and backed away, rubbing her palms down the sides of her habit. The old woman raised her voice, calling something in a strange guttural tongue. To Laurie's relief, Tarquin came strolling back from the shadow of one of the caravans with a tankard in his hand.

"That was a short fortune," he commented.

"I don't believe in such things," Laurie said stiffly.

"And time is passing. I have an appointment and my mother will expect you to put in an appearance for afternoon tea. Thank you, Mama Sarah." He bent and kissed the hand the old woman held out to him, tossed off the remainder of the ale in his tankard, then drew Laurie's hand through the crook of his arm.

"It would be better," he said as they walked back to the horses, "if you didn't mention our visit."

"I've no intention of doing so. My sisters would be very shocked, as would Aunt Marie."

"My mother would faint dead away," he agreed with a grin. "I suspect your sisters would be intrigued, but the Romanies are not to everyone's taste. I hoped they might interest you."

"They did," Laurie admitted unwillingly. "They obviously don't have any money or social standing, but they hold themselves so proudly."

"Why shouldn't they? The Bohannas have a longer and more honourable bloodline than you or I. Mama Sarah is a queen among her people. I hope she gave you a happy fortune."

"I didn't really pay attention." Laurie hastened her steps as she saw William approaching with the horses.

It had all been nonsense, of course, but how Mama Sarah had known about the man with the ruby on his hand Laurie couldn't begin to fathom.

6

CLARISSE HAD TO remind herself several times that she took no interest in worldly vanities when she saw her elder sisters in their Court dresses of white and silver, with ostrich plumes in their hair. Dora took the palm for beauty with her halo of golden curls and curvaceous figure, but Laurie also looked at her best. Her hair was plaited about her head, and her cheeks were flushed with unaccustomed excitement. Aunt Marie had been a little distressed about the girls' lack of jewellery, though not so distressed as to offer to lend them any of her own, deciding that their youth and charm compensated for the lack of gems.

The young women were only marginally more splendid than their escorts, who looked very handsome in knee breeches and embroidered waistcoats under tightly waisted coats and elaborately tied cravats. Aunt Marie, clad in lavender with a peacock feather fan, gave the four an appraising look and pronounced them fit to leave.

"Perhaps the Prince Regent will fall in love with you, Laurie," Clarisse said by way of farewell.

"He is more likely to fall in love with Dora," Laurie retorted. "She is a picture. Don't you think so, Cousin Tarquin?"

"All three of you look very well," was his comment, but his eyes rested longest upon Dora.

The carriage was roomy enough for the five of them, since skirts this year were narrow and none of them were fat. The whole procedure had been carefully explained to them by Simon, who couldn't resist repeating himself once they were bowling through the streets.

"The girls will stand in a line and as their names are called they walk up and make their curtseys, first to Queen Charlotte and then to the Prince. Two curtseys and a third as they back away. And you can't speak unless you are directly addressed."

"Oh, do stop," Dora begged. "You are making me quite nervous."

"My brother's post as junior equerry entitles him to pronounce on all questions of social etiquette, didn't you realise?" Tarquin said, straight-faced.

They were driving into the lamplit forecourt of the palace. There were other coaches as well, being directed into line, and flunkeys with large umbrellas assisted ladies in alighting. The younger ones wore the regulation white and silver, ostrich plumes swaying on their heads, while their chaperones favoured stronger colours.

Laurie wasn't sure exactly what she had expected, but the corridor into which they were shown was both cramped and draughty. Cloaks were being discarded, feathers fluffed out, and anxious chaperones were giving hurried last-minute instructions to their charges. The gentlemen had vanished through another door, and the air was thick with excited feminine whispering.

Somewhere beyond a curtained archway was heard a flourish of trumpets. A tall official banged a white rod on the floor rather in the manner of a drill sergeant calling a rebellious squad to attention, and the long line of white and silver began to move slowly into the vast panelled apartment where the Prince Regent occupied a large carved chair on a dais flanked by attendants.

"The Misses Laurentia and Theodora St. John, presented by their aunt, Mrs. Marie St. John."

Laurie's name on the herald's lips sounded as if it belonged to somebody else. She took the required number of steps forward, curtsied with her head slightly bent and her back straight in the manner that she and Dora had been practising for a week. As she raised her head she had a brief glimpse of a plump gentleman with the Order of the Garter across his chest and a thin, sharp-eyed lady with a long face and high tiara.

Rising, Laurie took a sidestep, kicking her short train aside, and sank down again. She was aware of a murmur of approval and wondered if it was for herself or Dora, then was making her third curtsey and walking cautiously backwards, her heart suddenly bumping for fear she might trip. Someone had touched her on the shoulder, and she turned gratefully to be passed into an even larger apartment where a string orchestra was playing in a gallery and servants circulated among the assembled guests with trays of refreshments.

"I was so nervous I almost died," one young lady was assuring her chaperone.

"So the ordeal is over, Cousin?" Tarquin had moved to Laurie's side. He handed her one of the goblets of champagne he was carrying.

"It was not so great an ordeal," she said with a smile. "I am quite sure that neither the Queen nor the Prince Regent would have noticed if we had fallen flat on our faces."

"On the contrary," he replied, "they are both much more observant than is generally realised. At a distance of fifty paces the Prince can spot a decoration worn incorrectly."

"I think he probably noticed Dora," she said. "She was quite the loveliest there."

"Indeed she is certainly attracting some considerable attention," he agreed, half turning towards where Dora stood surrounded by a coterie of young and not so young gentlemen. "She has a natural grace and charm that draws all eyes. Ah, but now we must keep our own eyes on the door. The Prince often joins his guests for a few minutes while they are having refreshments."

As he spoke the Prince himself, with his entourage, came into the room, pausing as those ladies nearest to him dipped into curtseys, and the gentlemen bowed.

"No formality, if you please." He had a light, pleasant voice, the voice of a more slender and attractive man. Laurie recalled that he had once been nicknamed Prince Florizel and had charmed the ladies.

She dipped hastily into a curtsey as the somewhat protuberant royal eye fell upon her, and heard the voice again at close hand.

"Miss Laurentia St. John, is it not? Your cousin is one of my equerries." He either had the royal memory for faces and names or was well primed.

"Yes, Your Highness. My cousin Simon has that honour," she said.

"You are a newcomer to London?"

"My cousins have come to winter with us from Hampshire," Tarquin said.

"You should spend a few weeks in Brighton," the Prince Regent advised. "It is quite my favourite place."

"Because Your Highness has made it fashionable," Laurie said.

"I realised that it had possibilities," he answered modestly. "You must bring your cousins to Brighton, my dear fellow. Now if you will pardon me I will drift onwards. One cannot always remain long in conversation with those one wishes to know better." He waved a plump white hand and drifted in Dora's direction, her admirers falling back politely as their royal host approached.

"Will you excuse me, Cousin, if I attend to Mama for a moment?" Tarquin was asking. "She has found some old acquaintances and will miss all the refreshments if they keep her talking."

"Yes, of course."

Laurie stepped back towards a window seat which was unoccupied. Being in a palace was less intimidating than she had expected. The Prince Regent had moved on from Dora and was chatting to another group. There was no sign of his mother, Queen Charlotte. Probably she left the social graces to her son. Laurie sipped her champagne and tried to take mental notes of the scene for Clarisse's later benefit.

The apartment in which the reception was taking place was elegant with its light panelled walls and gilded ceiling. She noticed in amusement that some of the servants passing round the refreshments looked haughtier than the guests. The ladies were splendidly clad in gowns so fashionable that Laurie began to feel grateful Aunt Marie had been so fussy about their wardrobes. The clothes being worn here reflected styles far more sophisticated than anything she had ever seen in the country. Materials were heavier and richer, with long tight sleeves descending from tiny shoulder puffs and skirts that were abundantly trimmed at the narrow hems. Many of the chaperones wore turbans pinned with brooches and decorated with feathers. She and Dora appeared to be among the few who were not bejewelled.

"You are surely not alone, Cousin?" Simon exclaimed, materialising at her side. "Allow me to fetch you some food. The caviar is always very good."

"I will take your word for it since I never tasted any of good or inferior quality." Laurie was amused at his look of pity.

"Never tasted caviar! I say, that won't do. I will bring you some directly."

He was back almost immediately with a plate of thin toast fingers smeared with what to Laurie's inexperienced eyes looked a little like the frog spawn Clarisse had once collected in the hope that it would turn into tadpoles and frogs and give Miss Browne a fright.

"Only take a little," Simon urged, "and you will marvel how you contrived to get through your life so far without it."

Trying to forget about the frog spawn, Laurie lifted a finger of toast to her mouth and bit off a piece. It tasted salty and fishy and she was certain that she would contrive to get through the rest of her life without it quite happily.

"Now if you take a sip of your champagne and roll it around your tongue, you will find how delightfully the flavours mingle," Simon said.

While doing as she was told, Laurie spotted Tarquin again, carving a determined path through the crowd to her sister's side. She took a second mouthful of toast and caviar and decided that it was better than her first opinion.

"It is a great pity there is to be no dancing," Simon was regretting, "but as it is less than twelve months since the Princess Charlotte died it is not yet permitted at Court. David, my dear fellow, I had no idea you were going to be here."

He addressed a newcomer who had drawn near and was bowing. Laurie took one glance and swallowed her piece of toast too hastily. In her entire life she had never seen so handsome a young man. His chestnut hair and dark eyes were a foil for features that would have been stigmatised as effeminate had their perfection not been mitigated by a determined jawline and tall, athletic frame.

"I was hoping to catch Prinny's eye, but he casts it resolutely everywhere," the young man said. "Will you not introduce me to your cousin? She is your cousin, is she not? I heard that your brother had returned to claim his estate."

"My sister seems to be occupied at this moment," Laurie said, pulling her wits together, "but I am sure that Cousin Tarquin will be happy to introduce you."

"I was angling for a closer acquaintance with yourself, ma'am," he said.

"With me?" Laurie wondered if the dark eyes could possibly be shortsighted. "Oh, I was under the impression that you wished to meet Dora."

"Later. As you say, she does appear to be occupied."

He glanced at Simon, who said promptly, "I do crave pardon. Laurie, this is my good friend David Cornwall, who comes too seldom to visit us. David, may I present my cousin, Miss Laurentia St. John."

"To whom you are feeding caviar when she would prefer to look at the portraits with me." David Cornwall relieved her of the plate and half-empty goblet of champagne, then drew her hand through his arm with an air of having known her for years.

"I shall leave you in good care, Cousin," Simon assured her and strolled off with a look that said he would find another young lady who required caviar.

"What portraits?" Laurie asked.

"Of the royal family. Don't you hang portraits of your relatives up at home?" David Cornwall enquired.

"I was brought up in a very modest country house," Laurie said frankly. "We were far too busy to sit for any artist, even had one ever come to the village."

"Busy doing what?" he wanted to know.

"All the occupations suitable for girls," she said, but broke off to exclaim as they entered a long, brilliantly lit gallery lined with portraits at which several other couples were also gazing.

"Something has surprised you?" His dark eyes were amused.

"These days almost everything seems to surprise me," she confessed. "I never realised how many relatives the royal family must have. Foolish of me, since Miss Browne was most insistent that we learn all the monarchs of England and Scotland by rote." She ended with a slightly nervous giggle so much unlike her usual calm demeanour that she was disgusted with herself. The young man would think her a half-wit.

The young man, however, threw back his chestnut head and laughed. "My tutor forced me to do the same," he said. "Very tedious, isn't it? Though some of our monarchs were not uninteresting. The Stuarts had a certain romantic charm which almost compensated for their complete lack of good sense when it came to governing."

"Someone might hear," she said.

"No Hanoverian ever objects to hearing his Stuart ancestors slandered," he assured her. "They don't even mind hearing one another slandered. What did you think of the Prince?"

"He seems very—charming," she stammered.

"And why not indeed? There is a vast amount of him to be charming. They say that he has been warned he may suffer heart damage from his appetite, but it makes no matter. When it comes to eating, our sacred Hanoverian line is full of courage."

"If you are heard, you may need the courage to face the Tower or some equally unpleasant fate," Laurie warned, half chuckling, half anxious.

"Then we'll talk of more savoury matters. Have you visited the Tower yet?"

"We have been nowhere save to church and the dressmaker's," she admitted.

"We, being yourself and your sister, Dora?"

"And Clarisse. She is not being presented until next year, but she needs to complete her education with some sight-seeing."

"So I shall have the pleasure of inviting not one, but three young ladies to visit the Tower with me?"

"Oh, good heavens, I wasn't hinting," said Laurie in dismay.

"I hoped so much that you were. I look forward to showing you some of the beauties of the city and also to showing you to the city, though I fear the latter will have the best of the bargain."

This was the kind of outrageous flirting against which Miss Browne had solemnly warned them all.

"If a young gentleman once gets it into his head that you are prepared to tolerate flirtation, my dears, you may depend upon it, he will speedily get other ideas as well. Flirting can injure the reputation of a young lady faster than almost anything."

What Miss Browne had neglected to mention was that flirting was also quite delightful. However, it was unlikely that she had ever looked at portraits with anyone as handsome as David Cornwall.

"If my aunt agrees," Laurie said at last, "it might be very pleasant to make up a party, but it will have to be after our coming-out ball."

"To which I shall beg for an invitation," he told her.

"If you're a friend of Simon's—"

"He is a year my junior but still an excellent friend. It looks as if you are already missed, for here comes your elder cousin with your sister upon his arm."

Tarquin and Dora would make a handsome couple as they walked down the aisle, Laurie thought, watching their approach—Dora's fairness against his black hair, her feminine curves with his hard, masculine outline. Laurie was glad that her own escort was so personable.

"It is of no use your trying to explain, Cousin," Dora was saying as they came up. "I could never get them all straight in my head—save for Alfred who burned the cakes, and there is no portrait of him here. Laurie, did you ever see such an elegant event? It is terribly tedious but very elegant."

"Your cousins are both originals," David Cornwall said.

"And the more precious in our family," Tarquin replied.

His voice and face had chilled, and his bow was stiff. It was almost impossible to imagine him laughing and talking with his Romany friends. No doubt he was jealous of the long look that David Cornwall bestowed upon Dora.

Laurie felt a trifle jealous herself and broke in. "Mr. Cornwall, may I introduce my sister, Miss Theodora St. John? I gather that you and my cousin are already acquainted."

"We are old acquaintances," said her escort. "Miss Dora, I am very happy to meet you and to congratulate you upon your debut. I suspect that the lovely Miss St. John will be taking the polite world by storm."

"That sounds rather fatiguing for my tastes," Dora smiled.

"Mr. Cornwall suggests that we all, Clarisse too, make up a party to visit the Tower," Laurie said. "I think it would be a most interesting excursion."

"That's where they chop heads off, isn't it?" Dora looked unhappy. "I don't think it would be a very cheerful outing."

"I promise you, they haven't chopped off any heads for a considerable time," David Cornwall assured her. "But if you prefer, we can take a boat downriver to Windsor. Parts of the castle are accessible to the public, even though the king is in residence."

Dora looked even more unhappy at the prospect of meeting a mad monarch.

"I think we must postpone any plans for outings until we have consulted with my mother," Tarquin said stiffly. "My cousins have their coming-out ball the day after tomorrow—"

"To which I have pleaded for an invitation, my dear Tarquin," the other added. "If you will excuse me, Miss St. John, I shall leave you in the hands of your cousin and sister and hurry to pay my respects to Mrs. St. John. I am certain she believed me still up in Scotland and therefore neglected to write my name on her guest list."

He raised Laurie's hand to his lips, bowed to Dora and Tarquin, who nodded brusquely in reply, and walked away, pausing briefly to greet another couple also viewing the portraits.

"That's an uncommonly beautiful young man!" Dora said so enthusiastically that Laurie gave her an alarmed look.

"He is a friend of Simon's," Tarquin said, offering his other arm to Laurie as they began to retrace their steps.

"But not of yours?" She looked up at him.

"His pleasures are not those which attract me. Simon is very fond of him, however. Cornwall is from an old, established family with Jacobite connections—back in the days when that meant something. He stands to inherit an earldom when his uncle dies."

"It seems to me," Dora put in, "that most people have to wait for someone to die before they get what they want."

"The entail on Gables," Laurie said, blushing scarlet, "was arranged by Grandfather. I cannot believe you mean to imply that Cousin Tarquin has been sitting for years waiting for Papa to die so that he could inherit."

"I wasn't implying anything at all, but it is true nevertheless. Now that king has a rather jolly face," Dora said, pointing at a portrait. "I would like to have known him. Who is it?"

"Henry the Eighth," Laurie said and felt rather than saw her cousin's hastily suppressed amusement. Dora appeared to much the best advantage when she was seated at a pianoforte.

They had reentered the huge apartment where the guests still circulated. Aunt Marie was deep in conversation with David Cornwall and her younger son and broke off to greet the rest of the party with a smile less frosty than any she had so far displayed.

"Mr. Cornwall has returned from Scotland," she said, "and is free for the night after tomorrow. I have warned him it is a modest affair but he declares that not even an investiture could keep him away. Isn't that fortunate?"

Tarquin looked as if he would have liked to ask for whom it was fortunate, but contented himself with a slight smile.

"And then there is to be a party made up for a trip to Windsor," Aunt Marie was continuing. "It is years since I was at Windsor, but Mr. Cornwall assures me it is quite safe to visit. His Majesty, God bless him, is confined in quite another part of the castle."

"If the weather continues so fine," Simon added, "we can picnic on the grounds."

"If there is any form of dining I dislike it is alfresco," Tarquin said somewhat sourly. "If we go to Windsor, we will eat like civilised people at an inn."

"Surely when you were in America you had to eat out

of doors?" David Cornwall asked.

"When it was necessary, but when I could avoid it I did so. Mama, I hate to cut short your evening, but it is getting late. It is bad tone to be the last guest at the party. Mr. Cornwall, we shall no doubt have the pleasure of your company very soon. Cousin Laurie, do you recall where the cloaks were left?"

"I have to attend the Prince," Simon said. "Will you excuse me? Cousin Laurie, Cousin Dora, this was a most agreeable evening."

"I too must pay my respects," his friend said. "Mrs. St. John, I am happy to have met you again. Upon my word, but I began to think there were three debutantes when I first laid eyes on you. I am still inclined to think so. One day, when I am a year or two older, you must tell me where you discovered the fountain of youth."

The bustle of departure prevented Laurie from noting her aunt's reaction to that fulsome compliment. She owned herself a trifle disappointed in the obvious lack of sincerity displayed by the charming Mr. Cornwall. Then she reminded herself that she was now in the polite world of Society, where compliments were prettily turned with little regard for veracity.

"A most successful evening," her aunt was saying when they were settled in the coach. "The Prince spent several minutes chatting to Dora. What in particular did he say?"

"That he hoped we would all go to Brighton in the spring," Dora said.

"That makes it practically a royal command then," Aunt Marie said. "We must rent a house there for a month or two, and the girls may very well be invited to all the functions."

By spring the house at Gables would have been renovated and repaired. The daisy and meadowsweet would be springing above grass freed from the grip of winter. The thought of Gables brought Laurie an almost physical pain. She lowered her gaze and sat silent, listening to her aunt run on. Meanwhile, the conviction strengthened in Laurie's mind that by spring, if her prayers were answered, they would be planning Dora's wedding to Tarquin, and there would be no need to go to Brighton after all.

== 7 ==

NEVER HAVING HAD a ball given for her before, Laurie couldn't tell if the preparations for this one were excessive, but when she chanced to think about the possible cost she quickly turned her mind to other things. The second floor of the St. John house consisted of two large apartments with dividing doors between, which could be folded back to create one room in which a dozen couples might stand up comfortably. With the furniture banished to the attics and small cane chairs set along the perimeter there was plenty of space. Late roses, velvety and long stemmed, were arranged in copper bowls on tiny tables; a third room was pressed into service as a supper room, and extra servants were engaged.

"A small and intimate affair," Clarisse said, mimicking her aunt. "No more than forty guests. We shall put card tables in the drawing room for the chaperones."

"Behave yourself," Laurie warned, "or I shall tell Aunt that you look a little feverish, and then you won't be allowed to attend."

That Clarisse was being permitted at the party represented a concession on the part of her elders, but Simon had pointed out reasonably that the sounds of revelry would prevent her from sleeping anyway. As it was understood that she would only dance with her cousins, the slight departure from custom could do no harm.

She would wear a simple white dress with a blue sash to denote her position as still a schoolgirl, while her sisters would wear the new gowns now shrouded under tissue in their wardrobes. Clarisse, who had affected to despise more worldly pursuits, had made surprisingly little fuss when told she also might attend. Laurie was beginning to hope that her sister's professed desire for a conventual life was fading, but when she hinted as much to Dora the latter shook her head.

"She is looking forward to eating the supper, that's all," Dora said. "She doesn't care about the rest of it."

Laurie wasn't sure she cared much herself. The advantages of living in the city were counterbalanced by a lack of freedom which irked her terribly, and she had never before become so tired from doing so little. She had hoped that Tarquin might ask her to ride again, but he was seldom at home. Besides, it was Dora she wanted him to marry.

David Cornwall would be coming to the party, and that cheered her despite Tarquin's coolness and her own instinctive disapproval of a man who tossed off compliments too easily. There would at least be a familiar face and someone who would dance with her. Laurie looked at the beribboned dance card and wondered if it would be filled up or half empty at the end of the evening.

The gowns she had described to Mattie looked beautiful when they were finally removed from their tissue shrouds and fitted onto Laurie and Dora. The blue and silver of Dora's dress emphasised her ripe fairness and Laurie's pink and gold made her look prettier than she had ever appeared to herself before.

"Now do remember, girls," Aunt Marie said, sweeping in with her lilac train rustling behind her. "Two dances with the same gentleman is the most that will satisfy decorum, and the first dance should be reserved for your cousins."

"Provided they ask," Clarisse said and was rewarded with a frown.

"I trust my sons know the correct manner in which to behave," Aunt Marie said then swept out again.

Laurie had wondered for years if her aunt considered it correct to ignore the existence of three motherless nieces throughout their childhoods. Now, she was beginning to realise that her aunt noticed only what was directly under her nose. Had her nieces lived in London, she would probably have taken an interest in them, but not until they were forced upon her attention did she bestir herself on their behalf.

"We had better go down," Dora said. She sounded as calm as if the vicar were coming for tea, a trait that Laurie envied.

Carriages were driving into the square and spilling out their occupants, and names were being announced. Laurie, standing next to her aunt, recognised several of the young ladies as having been at Court for their presentations. No doubt she and Dora would be going to their balls and supper parties, and the object of it all was to catch the most eligible of the young gentlemen and turn them into husbands.

"You look enchanting tonight, Miss St. John," one of the girls said shyly.

The speaker was a big-boned girl with a high colour who should not have worn yellow.

"Thank you, Miss—Darcy." Laurie remembered the name in time and wished she could return the compliment with sincerity, but she could only manage a weak comment. "Such a charming gown," she said, which made her sound like her aunt, who, having fulsomely greeted one lady, turned her head slightly to murmur, "Delia Trumpledor is the most tedious creature alive, but she sits on all the Charity Boards so one must be civil."

The music for the dancing was being provided by a string quartet at the far end of the room. As the first set began to form, Laurie was startled and somewhat dismayed to find Tarquin at her side.

"I believe it is customary to open the ball thus?" he said in answer to her glance.

"Yes, but I imagined that you would ask Dora," she

said.

"Simon is partnering Dora," Tarquin said. "Have you some particular objection to dancing with me?"

"No, of course not."

Blushing, she allowed him to lead her to her place, thinking that he would certainly be dancing with Dora later on. It was a great irritation that so far Dora had not evinced the least interest in him as a prospective husband.

"Our steps match well," he remarked as the measure began.

"I am a good dancer if my partner is expert."

Though taller and heavier than Simon, he was light-footed and held her with a gentle yet firm grasp that reduced her nervousness. Laurie stifled a tiny sigh without realising she did so, but that changed to a stifled exclamation when she noticed that Clarisse was also dancing—and with David Cornwall.

"Did I step on your toes?" Tarquin enquired.

"No, it is merely that my youngest sister promised she would only stand up with yourself or Simon, and now she is dancing with Mr. Cornwall. Aunt Marie will be displeased."

"I beg leave to doubt that," Tarquin said with a certain wryness of tone. "David Cornwall will inherit an earldom when his uncle dies."

It was the closest he had yet come to criticism of his mother, and Laurie could not avoid commenting on it as he swung her into a half turn.

"After your years abroad, you must often find Society tedious and artificial."

"Artificial, yes—tedious, never." He smiled down at her. The gravity of his habitual expression had vanished. "There are rules and regulations in every society, I assure you. The courting habits of the native Indian tribes are hedged round with restrictions."

"But they don't have prospective earls to contend with," said Laurie.

"The son of a war chief is reckoned a very eligible catch."

"You must find it a relief to be back in civilisation again."

"That depends on what standards one measures civilisation by."

"Is that why you go to the heath?" she ventured. "To contact a society with some of the exotic features that captivated you when you were in the Americas?"

"You are a perceptive young woman," was his only comment, but his dark eyes held her own for a moment which could have been uncomfortable had not the music ended.

"Miss St. John, I hope this next dance is free?"

Tarquin had moved away after escorting her to her chair. Now, David Cornwall took his place. He really was uncommonly handsome. His chestnut hair and bright dark eyes were allied to a white skin with a healthy glow upon the high cheekbones. There would be more than one fond mama eyeing him like a hungry shark, Laurie thought, and suppressed a chuckle as she handed him her card.

"There we are." He had pencilled his name for the next set which was beginning to form and for the one next to the last.

"You were dancing with my little sister," said Laurie as she rose.

"And she is not yet out." David Cornwall looked rueful. "Now I am to be well scolded for an act of pure charity. As there are three lovely St. Johns and only two cousins I declared myself an honorary relative so that the child might have the pleasure of a dance. Your aunt allowed it."

It crossed Laurie's mind that her aunt would have allowed almost anything from a young gentleman who was in line for an earldom. His action had been prompted by kindness, and Clarisse was sitting demurely among the chaperones once more. Meanwhile, he was a graceful dancer, though he had not the flair for making his partner feel more skilled than she really was, and once or twice Laurie almost stumbled when he slipped in a couple of fancy steps without warning.

"You have not forgotten about our outing to Windsor?" he said.

"I am looking forward to it," she said truthfully. "I have never been on a boat in my life, and I'm sure the castle itself will be most interesting."

"We must order fine weather too. There is quite a nip in the air now that the summer is almost over. I had hoped for a picnic, but Tarquin insists on dining at an inn."

"My cousin dislikes alfresco."

"And he is now master of the household." A smile robbed the words of sarcasm. "I would commiserate with you, but in my view the countryside's loss is the city's gain. If you had not come to London, I would never have had the pleasure of meeting you—or your charming sisters."

It was a pity that he showered compliments so glibly. It detracted somewhat from the pleasure they gave when she suspected she was not the only recipient of his gallant remarks. Nonetheless, he certainly appeared to be seeking her out and admiring her. Perhaps, if Tarquin saw her being courted by an eminently eligible gentleman, then he would be more likely to devote himself to Dora.

"My turn for a set," Simon declared as David Cornwall was leading her back to her place.

Simon had been dancing with Miss Trumpledor and there was a distinct air of relief at having discharged a social obligation written about him.

"You are wise to claim your cousin now, my dear fellow," David Cornwall said, "for I see a number of prospective partners waiting for a chance to inscribe their names in her book."

It was only a slight exaggeration, Laurie found. Having enjoyed a spirited polka with Simon which left no breath for conversation, she discovered that her little book soon contained a gratifying number of names. She suspected without the faintest twinge of jealousy that they had taken care to reserve their dances with Dora first, but at least Laurie was not condemned to sit among the chaperones with a stiff smile on her face. Tarquin came to claim her for the dance before supper, and she scolded herself silently for the way her heart leapt as he took her hand.

"Before you ask," he said, "Dora is dancing with David Cornwall, and Simon is partnering Clarisse, so you may step onto the floor with a clear conscience."

"Do you regard me as such a fusspot?" she enquired.

"I think you have an overdeveloped sense of duty where your sisters are concerned. I have noticed that before you stand up you glance anxiously towards both Dora and Clarisse to ensure that they are not being neglected."

"As the eldest I have always felt responsible for them," she excused herself. "I am naturally anxious that their lives may be happy."

"And now that you have been turned out of house and home by your wicked cousin, your anxieties have grown."

"The entail was not of your making, and I do not regard you as wicked."

"In what light do you regard me?" he asked.

She hesitated. The music was beginning, but Tarquin had stepped aside, drawing her into one of the window bays.

"Papa always spoke of you as reminding him of himself when young," she said at last. "He was the elder son, but he rebelled against convention while your father, although the younger, was more serious in character. I expected to meet a—not a rake exactly, but a—"

"A more exciting person than I turned out to be?"

"You make it sound dreadful," she reproached him.

"Not at all. Did it never occur to you that I might have

sown my wild oats in America and returned to England with the intention of settling down and fulfilling my duties?"

"I hope you do not number my sisters and myself among those duties."

"I assure you that I do. Pray don't tell me all over again that you have allowances and can make shift for yourselves. I may now own Gables but that does not mean that I would turn the three of you loose upon the world to fend for yourselves."

"You are most generous," she replied in confusion.

"As I never had any sisters," he told her, "all this is a novelty to me, and quite amusing."

"Amusing!" Laurie gave him an astonished look. "It is nothing more than a market, I assure you. The young ladies are displayed for the gentlemen to choose. I must confess that I enjoy wearing lovely new dresses and receiving compliments, but it is not in the least amusing."

"I suspect poor Mavis Trumpledor would agree with you." He lowered his voice. "I regret to tell you that this is her third Season, and her parents are in despair for she is past two and twenty and positively galloping into the sere and yellow."

Laurie was unable to contain her laughter. It pealed out, causing several people to glance in her direction.

"That's a vast improvement." Tarquin looked approving. "When you laugh, the line between your brows vanishes, and you look extremely pretty."

"My gratitude for the compliment, Cousin," she said and could not avoid dimpling.

"My gratitude for your company," he returned. "We seem to have stood up too late for the set. Shall we move into the supper room and secure congenial seats?"

It ought to have been Dora walking with him, but she was still dancing with David Cornwall.

The supper room looked inviting, with small tables and chairs placed in groups about the central tables where the servants were laying out last-minute dishes that had been chilling on the marble slabs of the pantry. The food had been described by Aunt Marie as light and modest. There was cold watercress soup, artichoke hearts filled with mushrooms, anchovy toasts swirled with whipped cream, oyster patties, potted crab with hot rolls, salads of beef and turkey, a poached salmon decorated with lemon, asparagus with a butter sauce, a variety of delicate tea creams and junkets, apple meringues and several fruit fools and, in the centre, an enormous trifle thick with silver balls and candied fruits.

"Clarisse will be in paradise," Laurie said as she surveyed the dainties.

Tarquin laughed. He had a pleasant laugh, she thought, and wondered if Dora had remarked it too.

"If Clarisse carries out her threat to renounce the world," he said, "she will have to give up culinary luxuries."

"You don't consider her intentions seriously?" She took a seat and watched him fill up two plates.

"Isn't it fashionable for young ladies to dream of taking the veil?"

"We never followed fashion," Laurie said. "I do assure you that my little sister is not accustomed to having whims. She may be only sixteen, but she has tremendous determination. I have never tried to turn her from her purpose, for that is the most certain way of sealing her resolve."

"The entire notion is ridiculous," he said, taking a seat opposite her. "Clarisse will make her debut next year and forget her nonsense."

"Clarisse may not," Laurie warned and dipped her spoon into the watercress soup.

Others were coming into supper, Dora with David Cornwall and Clarisse with Simon. It was kind of Simon to look after the younger girl, Laurie reflected, but she was less happy at seeing Dora with Mr. Cornwall, prospective earl or not.

"May we join you?" Simon had come over and was pulling up extra chairs. "I have promised Clarisse that I will choose her a supper fit for a queen—"

"Not a Queen Charlotte, I hope?" David Cornwall said. "Our beloved queen has many excellent qualities but she is frugal in her cuisine. Did you know, Miss St. John, that we are only indebted to her for apple charlotte because she insisted that all the stale bread in the royal kitchens must be used up?"

"Surely that is a canard!" Dora exclaimed.

"I was present," he said solemnly, "when she gave the order."

There was general laughter in which Tarquin didn't join. He made his disapproval of the younger man very obvious, and Laurie wondered why.

"Everything seems to be going quite splendidly," Aunt Marie announced, sailing in. "You must retire to your bed immediately after supper, Clarisse dear. We have already flouted convention sufficiently by having you attend."

"After supper," Clarisse said, eyeing her plate with relish, "I shall be too full to dance anyway."

"How do you contrive to remain so slim?" Dora said, nibbling cautiously at a bit of asparagus with an air of martyrdom. "It is a mystery I have tried to fathom since our childhood. I have only to look at a cake to gain weight while Clarisse and Laurie can eat as much as they choose without hurt."

"The more there is of your own fair self, Miss Dora, the more enriched the world shall be," David Cornwall assured her.

"Oh, do you really think so?" Dora looked pleased and faintly surprised.

"It astonishes me," said Tarquin, "how people can get away with talking a great deal of nonsense on social occasions."

It was an ill-humoured remark received by David Cornwall with a deprecating look and a raised eyebrow. Laurie could only assume that it arose from a jealousy that her cousin was as yet unwilling to admit and decided that he was probably half in love with Dora already. That being the case, she could help matters along by flirting with David Cornwall herself, a resolution she put immediately into effect.

"Does that comment mean, Mr. Cornwall, that the less you see of Clarisse and myself the better pleased you will be?" she asked.

"Caught, my dear fellow!" Simon cried.

"Not at all," the other returned. "Miss St. John is exactly the right size for her personality, as are her sisters. They are all three perfect of their kind."

"Perfection will take some living up to, I fear," Laurie said. "Will you not allow us one fault each, sir?"

"Only the crime of making all other women envious," he said, and raised his glass to her, his dark eyes sparkling.

"I had better check that Mama is comfortable," said Tarquin, pushing back his chair with an impatience that bordered on rudeness.

"Your brother thinks us trivial," David Cornwall said to Simon.

"Oh, he never had much small talk," Simon remarked easily. "He is the one who shoulders all the responsibilities in the family. Not that I wouldn't take my share, but he prefers to do everything himself without delegating. I assure you that since he came back from the Americas he has been a very dull dog."

"He has been very kind to us," Clarisse said with reproach in her voice.

"I am not slandering him," Simon explained. "He is an excellent brother, I promise you."

The conversation moved on to other subjects. Tarquin returned and went to some pains to address some polite, but noncommittal remarks which included David Cornwall, but Tarquin's earlier ease of manner had gone. The conversation having wandered onto music, Dora was earnestly begged to play.

"If it will not make you too nervous to perform before

so many people," David Cornwall said.

"Why should it?" Dora would not have recognised stage fright had it jumped up and bit her on the nose. "Cousin Tarquin insists that I practice every day, and I prefer playing where there are people to hear."

"We had better ask Aunt's permission," Laurie cautioned. "It is surely unusual for a young lady to perform at her coming-out ball."

"She just now left the room," Clarisse volunteered. "I saw one of the servants speak to her."

"I will go and ask her," said Laurie, then rose and left the supper party.

She felt a slight easing of tension once she was in the corridor. It was a pity that Tarquin's dislike of David Cornwall had to be so obvious, yet her cousin was making no attempt to charm her sister on his own behalf. If she remained away for a few minutes longer than was strictly necessary, he might pay Dora more marked attention.

Her aunt was not in the ballroom, where the string quartet were partaking their own share of the supper. Neither was she prinking in her own bedchamber.

Laurie went on down the stairs. There was a draught from the side door, which had been left ajar. She put out her hand to close it but was arrested by her aunt's voice, speaking in French. It was the first time she had heard Aunt Marie speak in her native tongue. Laurie had assumed that she avoided its use because it roused too many unhappy memories of the Revolution she had escaped. What struck Laurie now even more than the language her aunt was speaking in, however, was the tone of voice. Her customary well-bred cadences had turned hoarse and pleading.

"Je prie, Francois. Je prie," Aunt Marie was saying.

Too startled to realise that she was eavesdropping, Laurie pulled the door wider open till she could see her aunt's elegant outline in the light from the lantern over the door. A taller figure stood close to her, so close that one of his hands gripped her shoulder. The light gleamed on the large ruby which decorated that hand. That was all Laurie glimpsed before she softly closed the door again and fled back to the supper room.

= 8 =

THE BALL HAD ended at three in the morning and was generally agreed to have been a success, particularly as Dora had delighted the guests with a selection of traditional melodies. Aunt Marie had returned to the company just after Laurie and given permission for her niece to play. Only Laurie had been aware of the haunted look in her aunt's dark eyes. By the time the last carriage had driven away she was too weary to speculate as to the cause of the older woman's agitation but slept soundly until mid-morning, when Clarisse woke her with the information that every gentleman present had fallen madly in love with Dora.

"Except for Cousin Tarquin, of course. He admires you," the younger girl added.

"Does he indeed? He hides his feelings wondrously well then. I am glad of it, of course, for he and I would never suit. He is far too solemn for my tastes. Dora would liven him up splendidly but I wouldn't care to take the bother."

Clarisse looked unaccountably disappointed and went off to rouse Dora, leaving Laurie to decide that if Tarquin were developing a *tendresse* for herself it would have to be firmly discouraged. Dora was too pretty to be let loose in a world that took advantage of pretty women. She would be safer and happier wed to her cousin and sharing her time between Gables and the town house.

Laurie's modest inheritance would be sufficient for her

own needs, for she doubted very much if anyone would want to marry her. Then she recalled David Cornwall's compliments and could not repress a blush of pleasure. It was not likely that he was serious in the smallest degree, but his attentions were flattering and prevented her from thinking too deeply about Tarquin.

The presentation and the ball had provided the door through which Laurie and Dora entered the wider sphere of adulthood, though neither of them felt changed by the experience. A shower of invitations had arrived, each to be considered, then accepted with thanks or rejected with apologies.

The first engagement of any consequence was the river trip to Windsor, which had to be swiftly arranged before the weather became too cold. Accordingly, David Cornwall presented himself at the house on the afternoon following the ball, looking as fresh as if he had not danced every dance the previous night.

"The day after tomorrow would be the perfect time," he said, after making his bows. Only the three girls were present, Aunt Marie having sent down word that she was suffering from a megrim.

"Have you ordered fine weather?" Dora joked.

"Warm and dry with a slight breeze. I venture to add that the rain wouldn't dare to fall when three such young ladies are on the river."

"Am I to come too?" Clarisse looked pleased.

"You are supposed to be completing your education," Laurie said. "A visit to Windsor might be classified as history."

"Simon has no duties at Court that day and if Tarquin is also free—" Cornwall broke off as the latter entered the room.

"You have come to plan this famous cruise, I suppose?" was Tarquin's greeting. "I cannot think it such a wonderful notion to go sailing down the Thames at the start of autumn merely to gape at a castle that has stood and will continue to stand for hundreds of years. However, my own view is jaundiced, I daresay. Have you arranged about luncheon?"

"At the best inn in Windsor," David Cornwall said, with an air of propitiation.

"You will come with us, won't you?" Dora coaxed.

It seemed to Laurie that her cousin's manner softened perceptibly as he looked at Dora's pretty, pleading face.

"Certainly I'll come," he said. "Were the boat to capsize, I am the only one who has made the Atlantic crossing and would know what to do. There will be six of us—seven if my mother decides to make one of the party. She is not well after last night's excitements, but she will probably enjoy the trip."

"Seven then. Now we must contrive how to get the ladies down to the waterside."

"What a pother you make about a simple thing." Tarquin looked scornfully amused. "We will drive there, of course, or were you contemplating a race through the streets?"

"Your cousin likes to fun," David Cornwall said lightly, though his eyes showed less amusement. "We'll meet at nine o'clock then? It will be midday before we land at Windsor, and, with the evenings drawing in, the ladies won't wish to be out after dark."

There was general murmur of agreement after which the visitor took his leave. The younger girls accompanied him into the hall, still discussing the possibility of the weather's remaining warm, but Tarquin detained Laurie.

"Did anything occur last night to upset my mother?" he asked.

"Upset?" Laurie's mind had flown to the man with the ruby ring.

"I was under the impression that everything had gone off very well, but my mother only suffers from the megrim when she is emotionally upset. I noticed nothing amiss."

It was on the tip of Laurie's tongue to confide in him,

but a moment's reflection served to remind her that if Aunt Marie had wished her visitor to be known she would have talked about him.

"This is the first time that Aunt Marie has launched two nieces into Society," she said at last. "Perhaps the strain was greater than she anticipated."

"And how did it affect you?" He gave her his rare, unexpectedly warm smile.

"I slept late," she said, "but I was not nervous or strained. I couldn't help feeling the whole convention is rather foolish. Girls are supposed to make a few curtseys, wear some new dresses, and turn overnight into mature women."

"The marriage market." His smile revealed some cynicism now. "Cousin, I hope that none of you will consider yourselves obliged to accept the first offer simply because of the entail. You all have a home for as long as you require it."

"That's very generous of you," she said, understanding that the idea they might feel awkward about taking lifelong charity had never entered his head.

"It's good having you here." His eyes were still warm. "My mother felt uncomfortable about not taking any interest in you before and wished to make amends. I don't know if your father ever confided it to you, but he and my father were never close. Your parent thought mine was dull, and mine regarded yours as a ne'er-do-well. Without there being any open breach, communication between them virtually ceased."

"I believe my father resented the entail too," Laurie said, "though he never blamed you for it."

"And do you resent it?" He spoke gravely, the smile gone.

"I love Gables," she answered simply, "and it's hard to think of my home belonging to anyone else. Yet, there's no denying that the house is in a terribly run-down condition and it is good of you to spend money on it. With that and the expense of our coming-out I am surprised you don't resent the entail yourself. Your inheritance must be costing you a lot of money."

"Happily, my father squirrelled away his fortune, and I did well in America."

"But we are resolved not to be a burden for longer than we can help." She was determined to make that clear to him. "Dora is so lovely that she will have no difficulty in getting an offer."

"Dora will not, I trust, rush into wedlock out of gratitude."

There was a note in his voice that might have been jealousy, but before she could ponder it her sisters returned. Both had apparently decided that they wanted nothing more in the world than the opportunity of sailing downriver to Windsor Castle with David Cornwall. Tarquin took his own leave with an abruptness that suggested he had no desire to hear Mr. Cornwall's praises sung, and Laurie went up to her aunt's room to find out if there was anything she required.

Aunt Marie's bedchamber was where she frequently rested when visitors were not expected and when she desired to relax in a way that she was far too ladylike to indulge in in public—her feet up on a hassock, her hair uncurled, and a box of bonbons within dipping distance. This afternoon, however, when Laurie tapped and entered, the older woman was lying on the bed with a light coverlet over her. The face she turned to her niece in the half light looked ravaged by more than the gentle dissipations of the previous night.

"You have a bad migraine, ma'am!" Laurie's exclamation was concerned. "I came to see if there is anything I can do for you."

"It will pass." Aunt Marie sounded exhausted. "Was that Mr. Cornwall I heard below?"

"He called to arrange the trip to Windsor," Laurie said. "We assumed that you would be of the party, but you may not wish to go."

"Nonsense, I shall be perfectly well." Her aunt sat up,

reaching for the hand mirror. "I have a most resilient constitution. A trip downriver will be delightful provided the weather holds. Did Tarquin agree to the plans?"

"I believe my cousin regards the visit as a waste of time but is too good-humoured to deny the rest of us the pleasure," Laurie said.

"He disapproves of Mr. Cornwall," said Aunt Marie, putting down the mirror. "He considers him a—young puppy is the term I have heard him use. To be sure, Mr. Cornwall is on occasion somewhat frivolous, but he is a wealthy young man who has nobody to please except himself, and my own opinion is that he will settle down when he finds the right wife. He certainly seems very taken with you girls. It would be a splendid match for one of you."

"Our dowries are small," Laurie reminded her.

"Happily, Mr. Cornwall is rich enough not to have to make the dot the prime consideration in his choice of a bride."

"I wish such considerations were never necessary," said Laurie impulsively.

"My dear, you speak out of romantic inexperience. Wedlock is a serious affair to be entered into for many reasons, one of which is clearly personal preference, but that is by no means the yardstick by which marriage is to be measured."

"I suppose not." Laurie felt a little sinking of the heart. From the decided manner in which her aunt spoke, it was obvious that she would not regard a projected match between Dora and Tarquin as very desirable.

"I do believe that the worst of the headache is over. I think I will order the carriage and take a short drive. The fresh air will revive me better than any physic. Will you go down and tell William that I intend to take the air?"

"Do you wish for company?" Laurie paused on her way out. "I have been woefully lazy today and not set foot outside the house."

"No!" Her aunt's reply was so vehement that Laurie jumped.

"It was only a suggestion," she began.

"After an attack of the megrims I am very poor company indeed," Aunt Marie said in a more moderate tone. "I shall be quite well again by this evening. Ask Jane to come and help me dress on your way to William."

There was no point in forcing her company where it wasn't welcomed. Laurie gave the required orders and wandered back into the drawing room. From the upper rooms, now restored to their everyday condition, came the sound of Dora practising. Her sister had never taken so much trouble with her music before, Laurie reflected, but nobody had encouraged and praised her talent before Tarquin did.

"If music be the food of love," she said aloud, and was interrupted by Clarisse, who uncurled herself from the depths of an armchair.

"Shakespeare! *Midsummer Night's Dream!*" she cried triumphantly.

"Right poet, wrong play," Laurie said. "*Twelfth Night.*"

"It's a very foolish remark for anyone to make in or out of a play," Clarisse said. "I would like to see anyone try to digest a sonata."

"She does play beautifully," Laurie said, listening to the faint and melodious strains.

"Dora does everything beautifully. And without having to make much effort."

"While you and I have to work hard to make our mark." Laurie chuckled. "We shall be jealous soon if we continue in this vein."

"One couldn't possibly be jealous of Dora, for she is quite unconscious of the effect she produces. Where are you going?"

"For a turn in the park." Laurie felt suddenly restless. "Do you want to come?"

"The park only makes me more homesick for the country. Not that I'm trying to complain, of course, because when I enter a convent I shall have to accustom myself to living among strangers. I may even be sent out to the remotest corner of Africa. One is under strict obedience, you know."

She sounded so gloomy that Laurie couldn't avoid smiling, but the smile faded as she left the room. Clarisse's notion to enter a convent had not dissipated as had previous whims. Laurie wondered if her youngest sister's debut would have any effect, but that was a year ahead and Clarisse's resolve was strengthening.

Laurie took her pelisse from its hook and slipped through the side door. It might be considered highly unladylike to walk anywhere alone, but such activity had not been forbidden as absolutely unsafe. At this hour the park was till full of strolling couples, nursemaids out with their charges, and elderly people enjoying an hour's sunshine.

Seeing her aunt about to step into the carriage, Laurie hung back for a moment until the rattle of the wheels over the cobbles told her the other had gone to take her airing. She walked briskly across the square and down the alley to enter the park. Her spirits elevated as she smelt the heavy perfume of the late roses and felt the springy grass under her soles. It was not the countryside but would suffice until she would see Gables again. She wondered what her cousin intended to do with the place when the repairs were complete. Perhaps he would live in it for part of the year. Perhaps he would consent to letting her live there at a nominal rent, as a sort of housekeeper. Then, when he had married Dora, the two of them could come down and stay and Laurie could take a brief holiday elsewhere.

The picture of happy Tarquin and radiant Dora arriving to spend a few months at Gables didn't please Laurie as much as it might have. She had begun to ask herself why when everything else went out of her head at the unmistakable sight of Aunt Marie, minus carriage and William, in earnest conversation with a tall, heavily built man.

There was nothing to prove this was the same individual who had accosted Laurie or been found secretly conversing with her aunt on the previous evening. Nonetheless, the way in which he stood, with feet apart and wide shoulders slightly hunched, was familiar. Laurie stepped into a convenient arbour of shrubs to avoid being noticed.

This was the first time she had seen him in the light, and her reaction was one of surprise. He was older than she had imagined, on the wrong side of fifty. His dark hair greyed at the temples, and his face was heavily handsome with pouches of dissipation beneath the eyes. His clothes were not well cut, and there was about him the air of a person who has come down in the world.

Laurie was unable to see the face of her aunt, who stood with her back to her, but she could detect the tense set of the shoulders under the coat of ribbed silk. Though she stood too far off to distinguish more than the murmur of conversation, she guessed that it was not an amiable one.

Her aunt must have told William that she wished to take a turn in the park. Obviously, she had not encountered her companion by chance. The meeting must have been arranged the previous night, and the prospect of it had distressed her aunt into a migraine.

He uttered an impatient remark, half turning away. From where she stood, Laurie could see her aunt's hasty step forward with her hand outstretched to detain him. He had paused while Aunt Marie fumbled in her reticule. Something passed from her gloved hand to his. Then she turned abruptly and walked rapidly in the direction of the arbour where Laurie stood. For an instant, Laurie was certain she'd been seen, but Aunt Marie was clearly too preoccupied to notice anyone. On her face was a curious mixture of repugnance and relief as she walked to the open gates without stopping.

When Laurie glanced in the other direction the man had gone. She no longer felt the slightest inclination to walk in the park, but waited a moment or two before retracing her own footsteps. Luck was with her. The carriage was bowling in the opposite direction, and she was able to cross the square and enter through the side door without anybody being aware of her absence.

Dora was still practising, and Clarisse had joined her. Laurie, going upstairs to take off her pelisse, could hear the clear voices of her sisters. They sounded carefree, and she restrained a sudden pang of envy. Whatever was happening between their aunt and that man could not be confided to them or speculated about.

Laurie hung up her pelisse and smoothed down her neatly braided hair. Between the loops of soft brown her face looked slightly flushed. Her eyes were large, with the specks of silver almost crowding out the grey. Her eyes had always been her prettiest feature, but now she realised that her skin was clear, her features neat, her teeth even, her figure slender. She lacked Dora's spectacular loveliness and Clarisse's impish quality, but she was still a pretty young woman. A young woman with whom a man could fall in love. She shook her head at her own vanity and left the room, making her way towards the sound of the music.

Another figure stood at the half-open door, listening to the rippling notes. Tarquin had returned and now leaned against the door post, his dark head inclined. Through the gap she could see Dora's curvaceous figure bent over the keyboard, her fair curls aureoled by a shaft of late afternoon sunlight. Clarisse was dancing, her thin, agile frame darting in and out of view as she twirled to the melody her sister played.

Laurie felt as if she stood in the wings of a theatre, watching a play. Then Tarquin turned his head and nodded, making a beckoning motion with his hand. It seemed quite natural to join him and for him to put his arm casually about her shoulders as they watched and listened. It felt right, Laurie thought suddenly, as if they belonged together, but it was all wrong. Dora was the wife he ought to have. She was the lovely talented girl who would grace his home. Laurie moved abruptly away as the music ended and, clapping her hands, walked into the room.

"That was beautiful!" Her voice was pitched a shade high, and she wondered if anyone remarked it. "You really do have talent. What was the piece? I didn't recognise it."

"I composed it myself," Dora said.

"And I made up a dance," Clarisse informed them. "I'm not at all sure that I ought to dance when I'm going to renounce the world, but—"

"Don't you think it's time that you stopped this foolishness about renouncing everything?" Tarquin spoke in a tone of lazy amusement, precisely the tone guaranteed to inflame Clarisse's obstinacy.

"It is not nonsense!" Clarisse's cheeks flamed as red as her hair. "I have always wanted to enter a sisterhood."

"Since you were a baby in the cradle, I daresay?" His voice invited her to smile with him, but Clarisse's short-lived passions lasted twice as long if they were mocked.

"Since I reached the age of reason," she said stiffly. "It is a great waste of time to go to the expense of bringing me out, because I haven't the smallest intention of getting married. As soon as I am eighteen I will enter the Anglican community."

"If you are of the same mind when you are twenty-one, which I beg leave to doubt, then you will do as you please," Tarquin said, "but until then you are still a minor and can't go flinging your future away without my leave."

"You mean you'd try to stop me?" Clarisse was staring at him.

"I am your legal guardian, and I hope I have the good sense to make you wait until you are completely grown-up before you take responsibility for your whole future," he said.

This isn't the way to deal with her at all, Laurie thought, and sent her cousin an imploring glance which he either missed or chose not to acknowledge.

"You are threatening to ruin my life?" Clarisse asked.

"Three years in Society is scarcely what I would call ruining your life," he answered dryly.

"You are hoping that I'll fall in love and get married."

"If you don't, I'll drive you to the convent myself," he offered, "but meanwhile I do beg you to remember that you are still very much in the world and that you are growing up into a most attractive young lady."

If he had hoped to placate her with his final words, the attempt failed. Clarisse shot him a look of freezing disdain and announced haughtily, "If you will kindly excuse me I shall go to my room and pray for you."

Tarquin watched her exit. "She makes prayer sound like a threat. I had not thought her so serious," he said with a faintly troubled smile.

"Clarisse is always serious," Dora twisted round on the piano stool and flexed her fingers. "She wanted to keep a home for stray donkeys once, and after that she had a fancy to go on the stage. A touring company came to the next town, and Papa took us all there. Clarisse went round quoting from the play for quite six months afterwards."

"But this ambition has lasted for a longer time," Laurie said. "We make it a point never to discourage any of her ideas. Then they die a natural death."

"And if they don't?"

"That hasn't happened yet," Dora said, turning back to the keyboard and beginning to play again softly.

"Clarisse does not like to be forbidden," Laurie said.

"And I was somewhat tactless." Tarquin looked rueful and then shook his head, dismissing the subject. "I'll make my peace with her later, but I'll not mislead her into believing that I approve or will further her desire. Dora, will you play that piece for me again? It had an enchanting melody, but I thought the left-hand chords lacked precision."

His eyes were on Dora again as she played and Laurie slipped unnoticed from the room.

9

DAVID CORNWALL'S PREDICTIONS about the weather had been accurate. The morning of the expedition to Windsor proved bright and warm with only the merest breeze to add spice to the day. William, looking as gloomy as if they were all bound for a sail down the Amazon, had the carriage in the yard promptly after breakfast, and the ride to the waterside was taken through streets astir with early risers.

Aunt Marie came along after all, though she looked pale and strained, murmuring that her attack of migraine had affected her more than was customary. Laurie guessed it was more than headache that had etched circles beneath her aunt's eyes and caused her to use rouge with a somewhat lavish hand, but as she had not confided in Laurie, there was nothing she could do. Despite the older woman's determination to launch her nieces in the proper fashion and the care she had taken over the choosing of their wardrobes and arranging of their social activities, there was still a barrier between herself and them. Laurie suspected that, left to her own devices, Aunt Marie would have continued to ignore them, but that she followed Tarquin's requests in making herself agreeable to her nieces.

The boat proved to be larger than Laurie expected, with a small cabin where Aunt Marie could rest and a deck that was wide enough to be walked. Simon and David Cornwall were already there, and picnic baskets were being carried aboard, eliciting a sharp rebuke from Tarquin.

"I did stipulate that I won't sit in a draughty field to eat my luncheon!"

"These are to sustain us before luncheon, my dear fellow," David Cornwall assured him. Lemonade and white wine and patties of chicken and mushroom had been provided, together with a quantity of fruit. Clarisse, who had been quiet and sulky since the exchange with her cousin, brightened perceptibly and was soon helping David Cornwall to lay out the viands.

"The river looks lovely," said Dora in her placid fashion, leaning over the rail to gaze into the green-grey depths. "And it is not in the least chilly."

"It would be if you fell in," Simon teased.

"Why would I do that?" She gave him her sweet, faintly puzzled smile.

"It was only a jest," he assured her.

"Oh, a jest."

Dora smiled, and the uncharitable thought crossed Laurie's mind that, while her sister possessed excellent qualities, a sense of humour was not among them.

A rugged-looking individual was to sail the boat and made such a performance of pulling up anchor that one might have thought him preparing to cross the Atlantic. Laurie, whose own sense of humour was finely developed, escaped aft to conceal her amusement, leaving the others to settle themselves. Her aunt had shrouded herself in travelling blankets and was sipping lemonade while Simon and David Cornwall plied Clarisse with the dainties and Dora went on staring dreamily into the water.

"Is this your first time on the river?" Tarquin had approached and leaned on the rail within touching distance of Laurie's hand.

"My first time on any river," she told him. "We used to fish for minnows in the village stream when we were children and sail paper boats upon the pond, but that is the total of my nautical experience."

"What were you all like as children?"

"Oh, how can one know?" She frowned slightly, trying to fit herself in memory into a smaller skin.

"If I were to speculate," he said, "I would imagine that Clarisse was the one who roared the loudest and broke rules that nobody ever thought of making, and you were rather a solemn little girl, very conscious of being the eldest and responsible for the behaviour of your sisters."

"A little prig," she said lightly.

"Not at all. Prigs have no real sense of responsibility since that implies concern for others, and they are concerned only with the outward forms of conduct. I think you must have been a charming child."

"And Dora?"

"Dora was born beautiful," he said. "She was also born good-natured, so had no need to work at it."

"Papa always told us that you were a very wild young man." She had no wish to speak of Dora. "A kind of reprobate. Clearly, you have altered."

"I sowed my wild oats with a vengeance," he admitted. "My father packed me off to America in the hope that I might alter my ways. I trust that I have done so."

Too successfully, Laurie thought. She would have liked to meet the Tarquin who sowed wild oats. She recalled their visit to the Romany camp and wondered if he felt some unacknowledged nostalgia for the wildness of his youth.

"Your father was very cordial to me on the one occasion that I visited," he continued. "I regret to say that at sixteen I took absolutely no interest in little girls, so my memory of the three of you as children is exceedingly vague."

"Our fathers were never close. They were too dissimilar in temperament, I suppose."

"As are Simon and myself, but we generally get along well. He is a good-natured young man and well liked at Court, though I am not sure if the company with which the Regent surrounds himself is of the best."

"You do not approve of David Cornwall." She had lowered her voice, though nobody stood near.

"For good reason," he replied rather grimly but didn't go into detail.

"Do come and eat something," Clarisse begged, joining them. Her invitation was directed more towards her sister than her cousin, and there was a distinct frostiness in the glance she bestowed on him.

"I am still out of favour it seems," he remarked to Laurie.

"I do not like it when my ambitions are ignored and I am treated like a child," Clarisse said loftily.

"At sixteen you are a trifle immature to know exactly how your life should tend," he said. "If this ambition, as you call it, is genuine it will last until you are twenty-one when you can betake yourself to a nunnery, if not with my approval certainly with my consent."

"That's five years to wait!" Clarisse sounded as horrified as if it were fifty.

"You can fill up a five-year journal," he said heartlessly.

Clarisse gave him a look intended to annihilate and stalked off, her youthful frame rigid with outrage.

"You are not dealing with Clarisse in the proper manner," said Laurie, exasperated.

"I am behaving as any normal guardian would under the circumstances. The trouble is that Clarisse's whims and fancies have always been taken too seriously. She leads you and Dora round by the nose, and you can neither of you see it."

"While you, being unmarried and only recently returned from abroad, with no sisters and no experience of being a guardian, can see everything clearly, I suppose?" Laurie flushed with indignation.

"If you are going to quarrel with me too, then I will go and talk to Dora."

"Pray do! She agrees with me, but she would never be so impolite as to tell you so."

Laurie gave him an angry nod and followed Clarisse, feeling an unaccustomed pricking at the back of her eyes. She had looked forward to a pleasant day, and this small quarrel marred that. Again she reflected that it was a pity Cousin Tarquin had reformed so thoroughly.

She helped herself to mushroom patties and a glass of lemonade and went to sit with her aunt in the tiny cabin. With one side open, it was possible to enjoy the view but still evade the sea breezes.

"This is really quite pleasantly relaxing," Aunt Marie greeted her. "It is a long time since I was on a boat."

"It must have been very different when you came over from France at the time of the Revolution," Laurie began, but the other interrupted, holding up her hand.

"If you please, my dear, that is not a period I ever discuss. The entire subject is far too painful for me. For more than thirty years I have not allowed myself to think of those terrible days, or even to speak my native tongue. I pride myself on fluent, unaccented English, and I doubt if my old language would return easily to my lips though I willed it."

Yet, she had been speaking French to the man with the ruby ring when she met him in the yard.

Laurie made a murmuring sound that could be construed as an apology and turned the subject to the view. Certainly it was a pretty one as they left behind the high walls and towers of the city to glide on the swift current between banks thick with iris and sedge, past villages which clustered on the higher ground or meandered as if they too had adopted the contours of the river.

The sun was strengthening, gilding the boat and its occupants—turning Clarisse's hair to fire and Dora's to liquid gold. Clarisse had laid aside her ill humour and was chattering to David Cornwall, who was clearly taken with the liveliness of her personality. Tarquin was talking to Dora and evidently amusing her, since her pretty smile illumined her face. She had turned her back to the rail and was listening to him with flattering attention.

Which is exactly what I have been hoping for, Laurie told herself, and drew her gaze resolutely away.

It was almost noon when they came to the landing stage. Being agreed that the refreshments of which they had partaken had sliced the edge off their appetites, it was decided that the castle grounds should be explored before they repaired to the inn for lunch.

"I see no reason why we should keep together," Simon said as they disembarked. "We can meet up at the inn at—two o'clock?"

The suggestion was a sensible one. As there were seven in the party, Laurie felt obliged to keep pace with her aunt while Tarquin and Dora and Clarisse and David Cornwall walked on ahead. Simon, with splendid impartiality, flitted among all of them, coming finally to take Laurie's arm.

"There are seats under the castle walls where you might like to rest, Mama," he suggested.

"There is also a guided tour taking place," Aunt Marie said, indicating some people ahead within the main gates. "I believe I will go round the State Apartments with the guide and rest later. Do you wish to accompany me, Laurie?"

Good manners insisted that she comply, but Simon broke in. "Laurie's a country maid," he said, "and prefers parks to palaces. We will stroll about on the lawns until you finish your tour of inspection."

"Very well, dear." Aunt Marie cast an amiable smile upon her younger son and joined the guided party.

"You didn't really want to tramp round all those tedious apartments, did you?" Simon asked. "I've done equerry duty at Windsor and it's the dullest place you can picture. My mother will enjoy herself deciding how she would run the castle were she its chatelaine, and we shall enjoy ourselves more in the sunshine."

Laurie had to admit that the prospect of a stroll in the open air pleased her. For her, the worst deprivation of city life was the lack of real exercise and freedom. The lawns and gardens that stretched ahead of them were past their midsummer glory but far preferable to over-decorated rooms and passages.

"As a matter of fact, I wanted to talk to you," Simon said as they began to walk.

"Yes?" Laurie was surprised to see his lively young face so unusually serious.

"About Clarisse," he said.

"What about her?"

"Is she jesting when she says she intends to enter a convent?"

"No, she wouldn't jest about a thing like that," Laurie said. "There is a community of Anglican sisters near our village, and Clarisse often used to play in their garden when she was small. She has a romantic notion of what the life entails, but she certainly is not jesting."

"It would be a terrible shame for a lively girl like Clarisse to shut herself away in a convent. The truth is that I do rather admire her, Cousin Laurie."

"Good heavens!"

"Not that I'm the ideal partner," he went on hastily. "Apt to be a bit headstrong, you know. My brother disapproves of some of my friends. Bit straitlaced Tarquin is since he came home, feels it his duty to take his role as head of the family seriously. And I am fond of a flutter on the horses and so on. A good wife would steady me down."

"Clarisse is not yet out," Laurie reminded him.

"And when she comes out she'll have them buzzing round her like bees after honey," he said gloomily.

"Will she?" Laurie failed to see her little sister in the role of *femme fatale*.

"Inevitable," Simon assured her. "That auburn hair and the quick bright way she has of speaking. She'll be swamped. I rather hoped that you'd put in a word for me."

"I doubt if she'd listen. This notion of hers to go into a convent seems to be lasting a long time. Your brother made matters worse by forbidding it until she is twenty-one. Had he known my sister, he would have realised that the surest way to make her stubbornly determined to have her own will is to forbid her. And she is very young, for matrimony as well as perpetual chastity."

"But you wouldn't object if later on—?"

"Her dowry is very small," she felt bound to say.

"My father left me an inheritance, not as large as Tarquin's, but sufficient to manage on, provided I don't lose it. A fiancee would give me the incentive to save."

"A rich one would make that unnecessary," she countered.

"I thought of that," he said with disarming frankness, "but the truth is that since I laid eyes on Clarisse I can't seem to fancy anyone else."

"I would certainly not stand in your way, but I do beg you not to try to rush Clarisse into anything. At present the last thing on her mind is courtship."

"I'll be very tactful. You know the jockey who wins the race isn't the one who goes all out from the start. He holds back, gentles his mount along until the right psychological moment and then streaks ahead."

"I'm sure you're correct in that." Laurie couldn't help laughing. "However, I wish you had chosen a happier example. I have no wish to see my sister enter a convent and even less wish to see her married to a rake."

"Expenses at Court get a mite steep," he said sheepishly, "so when an opportunity comes to increase my allowance I take it."

"But you don't win every time, do you?"

"There's good and bad luck." He looked uncomfortable, and there was a note of relief in his voice as he exclaimed. "It's Clarisse and David. Shall we join them?"

Clarisse had recovered her good spirits and was laughing at something David Cornwall had said to her. As they came up, Laurie found herself studying her youngest sister with increased attention. Both she and Dora had always considered Clarisse to be the baby of the family when, in fact, only two years separated her from Laurie. At sixteen, Clarisse had begun to outgrow her coltishness. She was not a beauty, but her features—though irregular—were pleasing. Her hair was a striking and unusual shade. Beyond her physical appearance, her personality was lively and bound to attract. David Cornwall was making no secret of the fact that he found Clarisse amusing, and Laurie found herself grinning secretly as she was forced to consider the possibility that she had lost a potential admirer to her baby sister.

"Mr. Cornwall has been telling me such interesting tales about the goings-on here," Clarisse said. "King Charles the Second kept a suite of rooms in every one of his palaces for the mistress of the moment and—"

"It is history," Clarisse protested.

"I don't thing that the antics of King Charles and his mistresses come under the heading of proper history," Laurie began.

"Oh, don't be so missish!" Clarisse exclaimed, giggling. "You will gain a reputation as a prude if you look down your nose in that manner. Simon, you wish to hear the tale, don't you?"

Simon evidently did and, as they were approaching a path that made walking four abreast inconvenient, Laurie dropped behind.

"You three may talk over old scandals and leave me free to admire the scenery," she commented lightly.

Pretty as the scenery might be, however, her mind was not entirely on it as she lagged behind. Simon wanted to marry Clarisse and, judging by what she had witnessed, David Cornwall also had a liking, if not a *tendresse*, for the girl. The prospective nun had acquired two admirers before even making her debut.

Meanwhile, Tarquin had vanished with Dora as completely as if the woods had swallowed them up. Then, branching off onto a path that led her away from her erstwhile companions, Laurie caught a glimpse of Dora's blue skirt and heard her voice.

"I don't want Laurie to know yet. I wish it to remain a secret between the two of us for the moment."

"Your wish is my command, fair cousin," Tarquin answered.

He spoke in a teasing, affectionate voice such as he had never used to Laurie, but if she was not supposed to hear, then she had better turn aside. She did so hastily, walking rapidly until she was soon out of earshot. Back on the main path again, she slowed her steps and found herself regretting her own delicate scruples.

"Do hurry up!" Clarisse flitted towards her, her expression impatient. "We are going to collect Aunt and then walk to the inn for luncheon. Simon says it is not far."

"I'll look for Dora and Tarquin," Laurie offered.

The thought of Clarisse bursting upon them and possibly spoiling their secret by interrupting an embrace was to be avoided. The words were scarcely out, however, before Dora and Tarquin were glimpsed at the far end of the avenue, walking sedately and without touching. Clarisse sped off to fetch them. They all returned to await Aunt Marie's emergence from the State Apartments. Within a few minutes she did so, looking as if she had had quite enough of sight-seeing for one morning.

"The guide knew a very great deal," she informed them, "and he insisted on telling all of it."

"Shall I run and hire a barouche?" David Cornwall asked solicitously.

"If the inn is not far I will walk there at a steady pace," Aunt Marie said. "The air will refresh me. It was all exceedingly interesting, but too much knowledge can be a burden."

So can too little, Laurie thought, as they set off for the main gates. She wondered what Tarquin and Dora were concealing, but from the tone of her cousin's voice and the hue of her sister's cheeks she was afraid she had fathomed it already. It was exactly what she had planned.

Dora would make a beautiful wife. Clarisse would forget her desire to leave the world and instead turn Simon into a respectable and responsible husband. That left Laurie herself alone, unless David Cornwall turned his handsome head in her direction, but he was still talking to Clarisse.

The inn proved to be both comfortable and stylish. A private dining room had been reserved, and the food provided satisfied even Clarisse's hearty appetite. Conversation was desultory and general. Tarquin was clearly putting himself out to be cordial to his brother's friend. Dora was quiet as usual, but the glow in her cheeks and the sparkle of her eyes had to be caused by more than the exercise they had taken. Dora bore the appearance of a young woman in love, Laurie reflected, and both loved and envied her for it.

When the meal was over, Aunt Marie announced firmly that she refused to walk any farther until it was time to return to the boat.

"If you will instruct the landlord that I am not to be disturbed I will put my feet up and take a nap. With the curtains closed it will be almost like reclining in my own room at home, and then I can enjoy the sail this evening," she said.

Laurie offered to stay with her, but that suggestion was greeted by a shake of the head and the order to run along with the others and enjoy herself.

The interior of the castle having been vetoed, it was agreed that the town itself should be explored. The six of them set off, David Cornwall dropping back to walk with Laurie while Dora paired with Simon, and a somewhat reluctant Clarisse took Tarquin's arm.

"Your sister tells me that she intends to enter a convent," David Cornwall began.

"She is too young to have charge of her own future yet," Laurie told him, lowering her voice since the others were not far ahead. "My cousin made the mistake of forbidding her outright, which has merely hardened her determination. I am hoping that if the subject is not dwelt upon she will allow it to fade."

"Tarquin is apt to overplay his role as paterfamilias," David Cornwall observed.

Laurie was inclined to agree, but that would have savoured of disloyalty so she merely inclined her head.

"She is an amusing child," Cornwall continued. "I hope you did not feel yourself to have been neglected this morning. I was curious as to why she was at odds with Tarquin."

"I didn't feel in the least neglected," said Laurie, slightly indignant. "I hope you were not under the impression that your function was purely to entertain me."

"Not my function," he said in a low voice, "but my desire. I find you quite dangerously attractive, Miss St. John. One of the reasons for the attention I have been paying Clarisse was the hope that, if she were induced to like me, she might in the future plead my case with you. I will say no more at present, but I do beg you to remember that my interest is aroused. When that happens, my affections may soon be engaged."

He pressed her hand and lengthened his stride, forcing her to catch up with the others, who were looking into a shop window displaying a variety of fans. Laurie wished she had one in her hand right now that she might use it to conceal the bewilderment of her expression.

= 10 =

THE EXPEDITION TO Windsor had been pronounced a success even by Tarquin and a visit to the Tower was accordingly decided upon for the following week.

Aunt Marie, however, declared her intention of staying home this time.

"Places that were once prisons hold no appeal for me," she said. "With both your cousins to escort you and Mr. Cornwall to make up the party, a chaperone can be dispensed with."

Clarisse, on the other hand, with no memories of revolution to darken her past, was eagerly looking forward to the execution site and the block.

During the intervening days, there would be two coming-out balls to attend, an art exhibition to view, and calls to be made upon young ladies, making stilted conversation about trivialities while their chaperones sipped tea or coffee and decided privately that their own particular charge was the prettiest girl in the room.

Clarisse was excused from these social duties and, to Laurie's relief, betook herself to the extensive library at the back of the house, where she occupied herself in looking up references to past prisoners in the Tower. When she took her morning walk in the park with her sisters she regaled them with horror tales until Dora stopped up her ears and Laurie said dryly that by the time they reached the Tower there would be nothing left to find out.

It was astonishing how often in their strolls they chanced to meet David Cornwall. He was usually on horseback and always dismounted and insisted on accompanying them the rest of the way. She noticed that though he divided his conversation equally between them, he glanced most often in her direction, so often that even the unobservant Dora commented, "Mr. Cornwall is developing a *tendresse* for you, Laurie. Do you think you are wise to encourage it?"

"I don't encourage anything," Laurie answered in surprise. "Mr. Cornwall is very charming and attentive but I promise you that I don't regard him seriously and I doubt very much if he regards me seriously either."

"That's all right then," said Dora, looking unaccountably relieved.

Dora was a puzzle these days. Instead of being pleased at the prospect of her sister snaring a future earl, she seemed happy when Laurie had no admirers. It was not possible for her to be jealous even had her nature inclined that way, since of the two she was indisputably the greater social success. Her lovely face and amiable manner charmed the most trenchant mamas, and she was generally prevailed upon to play when they visited, with endless strings of young men eager to turn the pages of the music score or to join their deeper voices to her light soprano.

Laurie put the problem to the back of her mind while she dressed for the art exhibition. Aunt Marie was taking them since Tarquin had gone off on business. Simon had excused himself on the grounds that looking at pictures drove him crazy. Laurie suspected he was more interested in looking at the possibilities of a filly due to run at Newmarket. David Cornwall had mentioned the horse, and she hoped that Simon was not going to back it too heavily. His avowed intention to turn himself into a sedate husband for Clarisse had not lasted very long. It was true that he spent more evenings at home, but Clarisse remained innocently unaware that it was on her account. Her attitude towards Simon was no more than cousinly.

Autumn was closing in. The wind was edged with frost, and leaves scudded across the park. There had not yet been more than an occasional light shower of rain, though at this time of year Mattie's corns always predicted downpours. Thinking of Mattie made Laurie sigh. One letter had come, telling a great deal about the workmen who had descended upon Gables but nothing of Mattie's own feelings at being separated from her former charges. They were all growing up and growing apart, Laurie thought, and there was pain in that realisation.

The exhibition was to be well attended. They reached the main doors and were swept along in a crush of fashionably clad people, most of whom had probably come to be seen as much as to see. Acquaintances greeted Laurie as she struggled through to the first of the galleries and it became obvious that there was little chance of keeping their party together. She raised her eyebrows in the direction of the refreshment room and mimed a later meeting to her companions, then was caught up in the throng.

Pictures were a particular pleasure of hers as was drawing, though she was aware that her talent was small. Still, to look at the works of others was almost as satisfying as to have created something herself. She contrived to find a corner where the crush was thinnest and set her attention with some relief on the unframed canvasses that hung there. They were of varying quality, some imitative of the sweeping canvasses of David, others in the rustic melancholy manner of Poussin, but each one had its own charm. As always when she was absorbed, the rest of the world disappeared and she allowed herself to be drawn into the painted landscapes, her soul as well as her eyes registering their shapes and colours.

Someone bumped into her sharply, muttered an apology, and walked off as she turned round. It had been a grudging apology, she thought. Then she saw the man who had made it, pushing his way through to the gallery beyond the one in which she stood. The man with whom her aunt had twice met was an art lover, it seemed, unless he had come here to meet Aunt Marie again. Laurie was about to follow in the hope of gleaning some further knowledge, but, to her irritation, she was hailed by a decidedly insipid girl whose house they had taken tea at the previous day. By the time Laurie had extricated herself, the man was no longer in sight.

Her interest in the paintings had evaporated. She made her way with some difficulty toward the inner room, where the crush was lighter, but was again interrupted in her progress by her sister's urgent voice.

"Laurie, do come! Aunt Marie is having a fainting spell!"

Clarisse, whose experience of fainting spells was nil, seized Laurie's hand and pulled her towards the refreshment room, where two gentlemen were engaged in helping Aunt Marie onto a sofa while a third vainly entreated the crowds to stand back.

"Kindly allow me to pass. I am her niece." Laurie had raised her voice and was thrust to her aunt's side, where Dora was already chafing the invalid's hands and looking distressed.

"I believe she is having an attack of the vapours," she said as her elder sister arrived. "She was perfectly well. Then she became very white, clutched at her throat, and began to sink to the ground."

"Shall we run for a physician?" a gentleman asked.

"I think there will be no need." Laurie spoke rapidly, knowing that her aunt would be mortified by the commotion she had caused when she regained her senses.

"I have her vinaigrette bottle," Clarisse said helpfully. "Shall I wave it about?"

"Under her nose, not mine." Laurie saw with relief that her aunt's eyelids were starting to flutter. "The crowd was so close that she likely felt faint. A cup of strong tea might help if someone would be so kind, and if the people would cease pressing round."

The possibility of witnessing a heart attack at first hand having been denied them, those who had crowded forward to gape were persuaded to divert their attention and the two helpful gentlemen opened a nearby window. Another rushed up with a cup of steaming tea, then went at Laurie's request to find William and inform him that his mistress was unwell and would require assistance back to the carriage.

Meanwhile, Aunt Marie had feebly raised her head and was speaking in French. "C'est insupportable." Her voice was weak and terrified.

"You will be perfectly well in a few moments," Laurie interposed firmly, not wishing her aunt to let slip anything that might prove embarrassing later. "The crowd was too much for you, that is all. Sip this tea, and then William will take you home. You will feel quite yourself in a moment."

Laurie herself had risen to her feet, touching Dora lightly on the shoulder. "Can you and Clarisse contrive to assist here together? I have something I must do."

Without further explanation she made her way swiftly through the dwindling crowd to the main door. It had occurred to her that the strange man might have lingered to calculate the effect of his sudden appearance, and she was not disappointed. His tall, broad figure was just rounding the corner at the end of the street. Laurie hastened after him, having the sense not to run. If he did turn round he might see her following, but he never turned his head. When she reached the corner, it was to see him striding ahead up a side alley.

She slowed her pace, walking with her head lowered, her eyes flicking upwards from time to time to check that he was still in sight. It was possible that he knew by now who she was and would recognise her, but not likely that he would recall their first encounter. She wanted very much to know his identity and why he terrified her aunt so much.

He turned into a lodging house, bringing out a key as he went up the steps. He was staying in the district then. This was not, she realised suddenly, the most salubrious of neighbourhoods. She had forgotten that behind the wide main streets of the city were the alleys and yards where the poor lived huddled in their misery. This was not precisely a poverty-stricken area, but the paint was faded on the windowsills and a number of the fan lights were cracked. She hesitated, seeing a few yards off the swinging sign of a tavern. It might be possible to enquire there.

In her whole life she had never envisaged the day she would walk alone into a public tavern. Mattie would die of shock if she could see her now. Curiously, the thought of Mattie's horror steadied Laurie's nerves. She stepped to the door, pushed it open, and found herself in a low-ceilinged, somewhat dingy chamber, divided into booths rather like a stable. There was a high counter with racks of bottles behind it at the far end, but her courage only took her into the nearest booth, where she sat, shielded from view, wondering what to do next. The problem was solved for her by a man whose florid complexion suggested he enjoyed his own wares. He gave her a look almost as surprised as Mattie's might have been.

"Yes, miss?" His tone conveyed that she was definitely in the wrong place.

"A glass of lemonade, if you please," Laurie said nervously.

His expression readily conveyed his distaste at being asked for something as childish as lemonade. He went off to the high bar and, after much bending and puffing, produced a glass of the cordial.

He brought it to the deal table at which she had seated herself. "Are you sure you're in the right district, miss?"

"I am looking for a gentleman," Laurie began and blushed as the barman's look grew frostier.

"This is a respectable tavern," he said.

"I'm sure it is." Laurie took a deep breath and launched

into a hastily concocted tale. "I employed a man some time ago as coachman and neglected to pay him all the money that was due to him when he left. I chanced to catch sight of a man I am almost certain was he, going into a house on the other side of the road. The coachman was French," she added, sure that never in her life had she sounded more unconvincing.

"There is a French gentleman staying with Mrs. Briggs at number twenty-four," the barman informed her. "Monsieur Delmain. That was the name. He don't look like a coachman."

"Delmain? No, that was not the name. He did look very much like him, but then I only had a glimpse. Thank you. I will just finish my lemonade and go."

Laurie spoke with great dignity, but from the expression on the barman's face as he turned away she suspected that he had marked her down as crazy. She drank her lemonade as quickly as she could without actually gulping it, put some coins on the table, started to rise, then sat down again abruptly.

The other booths were not unoccupied. A couple of workmen sat at one table with foaming pints of ale in front of them, and a dark-haired gentleman had just entered through a side door and was ushering his companion to her seat. Companions, Laurie amended. The young woman had a shawled bundle in her arms. Laurie's first impulse to flee was succeeded by another of intense curiosity. She could not even begin to guess why her Cousin Tarquin was here in the company of a sallow-skinned girl with a baby in her arms.

Laurie knew she must not be seen, since she would find it impossible to give an explanation of her presence without involving her aunt. Unfortunately, the wooden sides of the booths muffled conversation. Laurie could hear only a low murmur from her cousin and nothing from the girl. Then suddenly the latter's voice rose.

"A baby needs a father. My little Tarquin needs a father!"

It was a rough, uncultured voice with a singsong accent that might have been Welsh. The words and not the voice were what mattered, however. Their import was shockingly clear. Even more clear was the clink of coin and the girl's breathless response: "That's ever so kind of you."

There was no point in staying any longer. If Tarquin and the girl were to leave by the front door, they would surely see her. Laurie took a furtive peep around the edge of her partition and, noting that the heads were turned away, left her booth and hurried into the street. She was too shaken to cast another glance at the house the Frenchman had entered but turned on her heel and almost ran back to the main road. To her intense relief, the first person she saw was William, on the driving seat of the carriage and looking anxiously about him.

"Miss Laurie!" Spotting her, he slowed the horses from a walk to a halt and jumped down to open the carriage door. "In all the excitement we drove off without you, and Mrs. St. John almost had another fainting attack when she realised it. She sent me to fetch you at once."

"Is my aunt better?" Laurie asked automatically as she stepped into the coach.

"It was the press of people all crowding to look at the pictures, miss. Seems a funny way to spend an afternoon to me," he answered disapprovingly.

"It's art," Laurie said and wondered what he would say if she told him where she had just been.

Usually the drive through the crowded streets would have irritated her since it was often quicker to go on foot, but now she was grateful for the interval. She needed time to compose herself, outwardly at least, though inside she was shocked.

Men were not angels, but, according to his own account, Tarquin had outgrown his early wildness. The girl had been holding a small baby. That child had obviously been born after his return from America. He had gone away as a reprobate and come back as a hypocrite. All that disapproval of Simon's gambling and Simon's friends had been a smoke screen for his own doings. It was useless to remind herself that he was at least giving the girl money.

The truth was that Laurie had been both disappointed and disillusioned. Somehow she expected better from the man she lov—the man she hoped Dora would marry. Laurie sat bolt upright in the carriage, staring out the carriage window but not seeing the streets through which William was slowly driving.

She was in love with Tarquin herself. Otherwise, the revelation of his behaviour would not have this power to shock her. She had convinced herself that he would make an excellent husband for her sister, when she had actually been falling in love with him herself. Now, she could not possibly try to change Dora's mind because she would be doing so for the wrong reasons. Yet, she could certainly not sit idly by as her sister fell in love with a man who had fathered a child out of wedlock, while setting himself up as a pillar of the community. Laurie was trapped in a dilemma that offered no easy way out.

She wished the journey home had been twice as long, but they were already trotting across the square, and one of the footmen was opening the front door.

"The mistress asks you to go straight up to her, miss," he informed her as she entered. Her aunt probably wished to scold her for vanishing. Laurie stifled a sigh and mounted the stairs to the bedchamber. She expected the older woman to be resting with her feet up but, instead, found her on those feet and pacing, with no trace in her countenance of her earlier faintness.

"Laurie, there you are!" Aunt Marie turned. "I fear we lost you in the crowd. I sent William back. Close the door."

Evidently, this was not going to be a scolding after all. Laurie closed the door and waited.

"You were present when I first regained my senses after my—fit of dizziness?" Aunt Marie asked sharply.

"Yes, Aunt. You were just coming round when I reached you."

"Did I say anything? I mean anything in particular?"

"No, Aunt. Nothing at all," Laurie said.

Laurie thought she heard a sigh of relief. When her aunt spoke again her voice was light and amused. "I would have been so embarrassed had I said anything out of place. You know when ladies are being revived from fainting fits or recovering from laudanum stupors after an operation they frequently say the most unladylike things—bits and pieces that they have heard and consciously forgotten. Some even use quite bad language."

"You didn't say anything at all," Laurie repeated.

"So my reputation is safe." Aunt Marie gave an unconvincing trill of laughter.

"Quite safe. Are you feeling better now?"

"Oh, perfectly well. I must remember never to attend another art exhibition on the first day. The crowds are really shocking. Thank you, dear."

For one instant Laurie was tempted to ask, "Who is the man called Delmain who frightens you so much? If you told me perhaps I might be able to help."

But her aunt kept her own counsel and Laurie did not feel she should force a confidence. Therefore, she smiled and went out again, closing the door softly behind her.

In the hall below Tarquin had just come in. She could see the crown of his dark head as he tossed his hat to the footman and hear his voice as he reacted to the news of his mother's fainting fit. Laurie could have gone swiftly to her own room. Instead, she found herself frozen to her place on the upper landing while he took the stairs two at a time.

"Is my mother all right?" he asked as he paused at the top of the stairs.

"The crush at the gallery was too much for her," Laurie said. "She is fully recovered." There must be something of the hypocrite in her as well that she could speak so calmly.

"It is not like her to do such a thing." He frowned slightly. "I have thought her a mite discomposed recently. Perhaps she is undertaking too much."

"We didn't ask to be presented and brought out in Society," Laurie retorted sharply.

"No, of course not. I was not imputing any blame." He looked mortified.

"Not that we are ungrateful."

"Gratitude is a cold companion." He gave her a somewhat rueful smile. "I cannot avoid sensing a certain resentment in your voice. I suspect that you would willingly exchange all of this social activity for a few months back at Gables."

"Which is now your property," she reminded him.

"A fact you find hard to accept." He stepped nearer, putting his hand on her arm. "I have been thinking about Gables. The fact that I inherited doesn't alter your bond with the home where you grew up. I hope that, in the future, you will continue to regard it as a home in the unlikely event of any of you remaining unwed."

"Thank you." She tried to speak coolly, but his hand seemed to have set her arm on fire. She would have been only mildly surprised to see flames erupting from it. He had proved himself to be a hypocrite, she told herself fiercely. He had seduced a girl who was obviously not of his class and paid her sums of money from time to time to ensure her silence.

"I will make certain Mama is feeling better." He removed his hand from her arm and turned away. Laurie rubbed the tingling flesh, scolded herself silently for being a weak-willed romantic female and went on down the stairs.

"There you are!" Clarisse darted out of the drawing room.

"Whenever you see me," Laurie said, amused, "you always look as if I am in the last place you would expect me to be."

"This time with reason," Clarisse said. "Dora and I both

fancied you lost and roaming the streets of London."

She was not far mistaken, Laurie thought wryly. "I was waiting for William to come back and pick me up," she said mildly. "Aunt appears to be quite recovered now."

"I am very glad that I am not an elderly lady in fragile health," Clarisse said.

"Yes indeed." Laurie shot her sister a quick glance and added innocently, "I believe the nuns have a lot of manual labour to undertake, so you will need to be physically strong."

"I am not afraid of hard work," said Clarisse with all the conviction of someone who has never done any.

"And on a plain diet. I don't envy you." Laurie broke off as Dora joined them.

"You were not run over or abducted then," she said placidly. "I insisted you were not."

"My mother is well again." Tarquin's voice sounded above them. "She will eat dinner in her room, so we are to contrive without her. Dora, I have something to speak to you about."

"Coming." Dora's pretty face lit up, and she almost ran up the staircase.

"I hope nothing is wrong." Laurie looked after her.

"Oh, it will be more secrets, I expect," Clarisse said, drifting back into the drawing room.

"Secrets?" There was no reason for Laurie to catch her breath as if she felt a sudden pang.

"They are always having secrets together," said Clarisse. "Haven't you noticed?"

Her voice was cheerfully indifferent, but Laurie felt the pang again, even sharper than before.

= 11 =

THE MORNING OF their visit to the Tower was chilly, with a pale sun struggling through banks of cloud. David Cornwall, however, prophesied that the rain would hold off.

"Even if it were to shower," he said, "we will be under cover most of the time. There are so many interesting things to see."

"The block and the axe," Clarisse said promptly.

Her sisters looked pained at her ghoulish taste, but David Cornwall laughed.

"I will escort you there myself if the others don't wish to see it," he promised.

"I would like the menagerie," Laurie said. "I never saw a real lion in my life."

Dora, who was inclined to be timid, declared she was most interested in the Crown Jewels.

"It would be wonderful to try them on," she said wistfully.

"Your beauty would diminish them," David Cornwall promptly added.

Too promptly, thought Laurie.

"If we are all ready—?" There was a trace of impatience in Tarquin's voice, or it could be jealousy. He might resent other men, particularly one whom he didn't like, noticing Dora's beauty.

David Cornwall had brought his own curricle, and nothing would satisfy Clarisse but that she be allowed to ride in it.

"I hate sitting in a stuffy carriage," she complained, "and I may never get another opportunity to ride in such a vehicle."

"I doubt if they'll go out of fashion in the next few years," Tarquin said dryly. "If you drive at a civilised pace, Cornwall?"

"Like an old lady with broken spectacles," the other promised.

Clarisse uttered a whoop of delight, which she hastily suppressed, and went to board the high, narrow passenger seat, while the remaining four entered the coach.

"It is kind of him to indulge her whim," Laurie said to Tarquin, but received a frown in return.

"He indulges his own whims often enough."

"My brother considers him a bad influence on my character," Simon said. "If I were under age he would forbid David the house."

"Oh, do let us be comfortable together," Dora implored. "We had the most tedious visit yesterday to the Winters', and I was almost asleep by the time we left. I was looking forward to today."

"It is a pity that Aunt Marie didn't accompany us. She might have found the trip of interest despite its sad associations," Laurie said.

"She lost all her relatives in the Revolution. Anything that savours of prisons or executions upsets her," Tarquin said. "She is not well either. I think we ought to persuade her to consult her physician, Simon."

"She is probably annoyed at losing her brooch," his brother said.

"What brooch? I didn't know she had lost anything."

"She asked me not to mention it." Simon bit his lip. "When she was dressing for dinner last evening she had on that grey dress. She looked a little pale, and I suggested she put on the diamond brooch that Papa gave her for their anniversary. At first she said she didn't feel like wearing diamonds when we were just eating *en famille* and then she admitted she had lost the brooch but cannot recall where. The clasp was loose, she said."

"That was a valuable piece of jewellery," Tarquin said. "I wish she had mentioned it so we could have begun a search."

"I cannot remember Aunt wearing a diamond brooch," Dora said.

"It was shaped like a fern leaf, with the diamonds set in gold," Tarquin told her. "I always admired that piece. My father had excellent taste."

Laurie sat very still in her corner of the carriage and wondered how to change the topic of conversation without being too obvious. It was plain to her that her aunt had given the jewel to the man with the ruby ring, which meant that he was being paid—but for what? His silence perhaps? She speculated as to whether Aunt Marie could possibly have a lover, but that seemed in the last degree unlikely. Her pleading tone of voice in the yard had been that of a frightened woman, not one enjoying a *liaison*.

They had reached the slope leading to the Tower entrance. As they alighted, David Cornwall drove up with exaggerated care. Clarisse beamed as she scrambled out.

"A curricle is the only way to travel," she declared. "Mr. Cornwall would not let me take the reins, though."

"Then he shows good sense," Tarquin said, giving the other a glance of grudging approval.

"You never handled anything faster than a pony trap in your life," Laurie scolded. "I hope you didn't make a bother of yourself."

Clarisse's eyes flashed more green than grey. "When are you going to realise that I'm not a baby?" she demanded. "I'm only two years younger than you, for heaven's sake."

"Laurie didn't like to think of you landing in a ditch," Dora said peaceably.

"You're right, and I'm being a brat." Clarisse's flash of temper vanished in contriteness. She put her arms round

Laurie, hugging her so fiercely that the older girl was startled.

"Now that hostilities have ceased shall we buy our tickets?" Tarquin enquired, moving towards the stone arches that spanned the entrance.

The day had been dull, but even now, with the clouds dispersing and the sun triumphing, the walls of the ancient state prison had a forbidding look. As she paced along the cobbled walk between the towers of dark stone, Laurie was conscious that many who had come here in the past had been not visitors but prisoners. And not all of them had walked free again.

"That's Traitor's Gate." Clarisse was hanging over the low parapet. "They used to bring prisoners by water and they knew when the boat landed at the steps that they probably would never see the outside world again."

"Like nuns," Simon added tactlessly, but Clarisse was too busy airing the knowledge she had gleaned from her recent bout of reading to pay attention.

"Elizabeth the First was brought this way when her sister put her in prison. She got out in the end, though, and became queen. Isn't that a terrible thing for one sister to do to another?"

"Would you ever do that, Laurie, if you were queen?" Dora enquired.

The thought ran through Laurie's mind that at least here her sisters would be safe. It was an odd thought to strike her, for there was nothing to threaten them. Yet the feeling remained.

"Are we going to stay together all the time?" Simon was asking. "It might be more amusing to separate and meet for luncheon to compare notes."

This was voted the most sensible course. Tarquin offered Laurie his arm with the comment that live lions interested him more than dead jewels. Simon would take Dora to the jewel house and David Cornwall agreed to indulge Clarisse in her taste for horrors.

"It is very good of him to pay attention to her," Laurie

remarked as she and Tarquin walked towards the Lion Tower. "She is at that difficult age between child and young lady."

"You and Dora having reached your middle years, I suppose?" His voice was teasing, and the smile in his dark eyes made her forget that she was shocked by his behaviour.

"I have always been considered rather mature for my years," she answered. "Not having a mother and with Papa away so much of the time I felt responsible. I find it hard to relinquish that."

"And I find it hard to act like a guardian to three young ladies who are only a decade younger than myself," he confessed. "I try to behave very correctly, the way my own father always acted, but there are times when I hear myself scolding Simon for losing money on cards or horses and remember myself at that same age."

He was trying to convince her that he was a reformed and responsible person, but she had seen the girl with the baby. Something inside Laurie chilled. Fortunately, they had arrived at the steps that led down to the lion's den, and she was able to slip her hand out of the crook of his arm and stand at the guarding rail, her face eager with interest as the tawny-maned creature paced, with endlessly swishing tail, beyond the high bars.

"He would prefer to be back in his jungle," she said at last.

"And what of you, Laurie? Would you prefer to be back at Gables?"

His question took her by surprise. Just as she resolved to treat him with cold courtesy, reserving judgement on his private life, he asked her something in a tone that suggested he really cared about her answer.

"I'm looking forward to going back there in the spring," she admitted. "I know it might not seem very exciting to you, but it was my home. It was always safe there."

"Safe?" he echoed, taking her hand as they turned to mount the steps again.

"It's a strange word to use, I know." She hesitated. "My father was seldom home, you see, and as a child I always had the fear that one day he would go off on one of his visits and never return. On the other hand, I enjoyed being mistress of the house. It gave me a certain authority."

"Over your sisters?"

"I want what's best for both of them," she said defensively. "I don't want them to be hurt."

"You can't keep Dora a child forever. She's your contemporary."

"I want Dora to be happy." She glanced at him, wondering how much she could safely say.

"By your lights, or hers?"

"I want her to marry a man who will cherish her and not have any dark places in his life," she said, then walked on ahead towards the raven cages that bordered the green.

She was glad to see Dora and Simon approaching. The conversation with her cousin had been unsettling and too full of unfinished thoughts.

"We took one quick look at the Crown Jewels and came to fetch you," Dora said. "You must see them, Laurie. They are absolutely magnificent."

Tarquin's eyes rested on Dora's lovely face with pleasure. Perhaps, his affair with the girl in the tavern had been only a passing fancy, Laurie thought, and he would prove a model husband. Whatever happened, she had no right in the world to stand in the way of her sister's potential happiness.

They went to look at the jewels, kept temptingly out of reach behind glass. They were indeed magnificent, but there were too many of them, Laurie thought. Everything was too thickly encrusted with precious stones. So much gold and silver made her eyes ache. When they came out it was to find David Cornwall hurrying towards them, a look of concern on his face.

"What's happened?" she exclaimed.

"Clarisse twisted her ankle," he said. "She wanted to go up one of the spiral staircases, and coming down she slipped. It isn't serious, but it does look like a bad sprain. I was coming to find you to tell you that I'll take her home and ask your aunt to get the doctor."

"Where is Clarisse?" Tarquin asked.

"Over there, seated on the steps." David Cornwall waved a hand. "She really is not badly hurt, but she is upset at spoiling the day for you."

Clarisse indeed looked more guilty than hurt when they reached her. She was massaging her foot and looked up with a slightly wobbly smile.

"It isn't even swollen," she said, "but it hurts when I put any weight on it. Mr. Cornwall has kindly offered to take me home—"

"We'll all go, of course," Laurie began, but Clarisse shook her red head.

"I'd hate to ruin everyone's day out," she protested. "Honestly, I'd be much happier just going home. Aunt Marie can call the doctor if necessary. You can tell me all about everything else after."

"If you're sure," Laurie said doubtfully, and David Cornwall chimed in. "I can take her back, then drive to fetch the doctor myself."

"If your ankle isn't swollen you may have broken a small bone in it," Tarquin warned.

"I'll carry you to the curricle," Simon offered, looking more pleased than otherwise at the prospect of holding his cousin in his arms.

"I simply don't want a fuss," Clarisse said.

She sounded suddenly close to tears, of embarrassment rather than pain, Laurie thought, which was odd since her youngest sister generally did not object to being the centre of attention.

"We'll wait here," said Laurie soothingly. "There's no virtue in making a procession out of it. You can see the rest on another occasion. At least you got to look at the block and the axe, I hope?"

"They were marvellously gruesome," Clarisse said, brightening as Simon picked her up to carry her towards the entrance.

"She is not usually such a baby," Dora mused.

"Disappointed, I expect. Tarquin, do you think one of us ought to go back with her to explain to Aunt?" Laurie asked.

"I'm sure Mr. Cornwall will do that," Dora said. "Poor Clarisse! She will be miffed at having her tour cut short. I don't suppose she contrived to see any of the instruments of torture."

Simon was with them again in a few moments, looking rather flushed.

"She has heavy bones, I think," he said feelingly. "I perched her in the passenger seat, and David is driving her by the shortest route, so I think she will soon have the advice of a doctor. She was not in much pain."

"It was careless of your friend to allow her to slip," Tarquin said.

"You can't blame David for an accident," Simon reproached. "Hanged if I can make out what the deuce you have against him apart from the fact he doesn't object to losing a little money sometimes."

"Especially if it happens to be someone else's money," Tarquin said, then held up his hands in a gesture of surrender. "Very well, we will agree to differ about the relative virtues and vices of Mr. Cornwall. Now shall we go and look at the armouries?"

They had changed places again, Tarquin moving ahead with Dora's hand tucked under his arm while Simon followed with Laurie. It was like a quadrille, she thought, but one in which she was not completely certain of the steps. She had expected to despise Tarquin after the revelation in the tavern, but she could not, no matter how firmly she told herself that he was a whited sepulchre. Whoever the girl had been, she was clearly not of his class, and he did at least give her financial support of some kind.

"If King Henry the Eighth was really so enormous it's

no wonder his courtiers were terrified of him," Simon remarked. "On the other hand, Anne Boleyn did cut off his head."

"What?" Laurie blinked at him. "In all the history books they have it the other way round."

"I merely wanted to find out if you were paying attention," he grinned. "You have been walking about with a look on your face that makes me suspect you are a thousand miles away."

"I'm sorry. I fear I am dull company," she apologised. "I was thinking of other matters."

"So was I," he said ruefully. "I hope Clarisse's ankle is not too badly hurt. You know, there were tears in her eyes when I lifted her into the curricle."

"I feel we ought to cut the expedition short," Laurie confessed, "but I am sure that a doctor will have been procured by now. Clarisse will feel badly if we return early on her account."

"And Tarquin and Dora are clearly enjoying themselves," Simon added.

Laurie's gaze flew to the other side of the huge apartment. Her sister and cousin had paused before a glass showcase displaying some tiny suits of armour designed for young boys, but they seemed more intent on each other than on the exhibits. They stood close, Dora's pretty face tilted upwards as she listened to something Tarquin was saying to her. She looked, even at a distance, utterly happy and content.

"Shall we eat luncheon?" Simon suggested, breaking into her thoughts.

Laurie agreed, but could not avoid noticing the quick blush that came and went in her sister's cheeks as the conversation with Tarquin ended.

The inn where a midday meal had been ordered was within walking distance of the Tower gates. The food was excellent, but Laurie could not savour it as much as was deserved. She told herself she was fretting over Clarisse, who would have relished the oysters, the beef *medaillons*, and the syllabub. The truth was closer, however, as close as Dora sitting next to Tarquin, gazing at him in a manner Laurie would have termed flirtatious in any other young lady.

After the lunch, a river trip from the Tower Wharf to the Palace of Westminster was agreed upon. William had firmly declined a ticket to view the Tower and could drive to Westminster and meet them there for the ride home. The two young ladies, one in a far happier frame of mind than the other, were escorted aboard the barge by their escorts, and the grim walls of the State Prison diminished into the distance as the vessel ploughed through the grey waters of the Thames.

The guide on the barge at once began his monologue, pointing out the site of the ancient Globe theatre and the old Southwark district, which had once been a place of sanctuary, and she was relieved when the short voyage was over and they stepped out onto the embankment. The carved Gothic facade of Westminster Hall distracted her briefly. It was so like the picture of it she had conceived in her mind. Still, she could not pretend much disappointment when a few large drops of rain unexpectedly splashed down out of a sky overcast by clouds again, and William came bowling up with the carriage.

"I hope Clarisse is feeling more the thing," Simon said as they seated themselves inside. He sounded concerned. Obviously his *tendresse* for her little sister was no passing fancy.

"She will be waiting to hear all about what we saw," Dora answered. "Clarisse has a marvellous capacity for pleasure, even at secondhand."

As I have for misery, thought Laurie and gave herself a brisk mental shake. It had been her fondest desire that her sister would be safely wed to Tarquin and thus enabled to live at Gables for at least part of the year. If Tarquin was not exactly the pillar of rectitude he professed to be, he was surely no worse than many young men led astray by a pretty face. Now, Clarisse would forget her ambition to renounce the world and look with fresh appreciation at Simon. And I, Laurie decided, will make a splendid maiden aunt unless I marry David Cornwall, who appears to have forgotten his first interest in me.

The rain was coming down in fine needles by the time they reached the house. The girls covered their heads with their pelisses as they ran up the steps to the door which Thomas was holding open.

"Were you caught in the rain?" Aunt Marie's voice came from the drawing room above. "I meant to remind you to take umbrellas."

"Is Clarisse feeling better?" Simon was bounding up the stairs.

"Is she sick?" Aunt Marie's slender figure appeared at the top of the staircase. "You probably pressed her to eat something too rich at luncheon."

"She slipped and sprained her ankle. Isn't she here?" Laurie felt a sudden churning in her stomach.

"She was with you. Didn't you come home together?" Her aunt sounded bewildered.

"Mr. Cornwall brought her home in the curricle hours ago," Dora said.

"There must have been an accident." Simon's face whitened.

"No, wait."

Laurie hurried up the stairs; the churning had turned to panic and—unbearable suspicion.

She took the second flight of stairs at a run and opened the door to Clarisse's bedroom. It was as neat as usual, her youngest sister having escaped Dora's habits of cheerful untidiness. It took only a moment for her eyes to discern the folded sheet of paper tucked behind the clock.

Clarisse's round, schoolgirl hand stared up at Laurie as she unfolded the message and went down the stairs again. The others had joined Aunt Marie and Simon in the upper hall and gazed in perplexity as if Laurie had taken leave of her senses.

"You look dreadful," said Dora shakily.

"Clarisse left a note," Laurie said. The writing blurred before her eyes, then was clear again as she read aloud.

> Dear Laurie and Dora,
> This is a very hard letter to write, but I don't want to wait five years before I go into the convent. To have me presented and brought out would be a big expense and a waste of money. Mr. Cornwall agrees with me and has offered to help. By the time you read this I will probably be in St. Cecilia's. I will write to you from there. Do try to understand and forgive me.
> Your loving sister,
> Clarisse St. John.

=12=

AFTER THE READING of the letter there was chaos. Aunt Marie fainted for the second time in a week, and Dora burst into tears while Tarquin and Simon shouted at each other. Oddly enough, though Laurie was as shocked as any of them, she maintained sufficient presence of mind to call for Jane to revive her aunt. Laurie then provided the weeping Dora with a handkerchief and demanded that her cousins stop blaming each other and take some action.

"Where is this St. Cecilia's?" Simon wanted to know.

"Just outside our village," Laurie told him. "They cannot reach it before tonight."

"He will not have taken her in the curricle." Tarquin had controlled his temper, but his face was dark. "In this rain they will have gone on in a closed carriage, which means he will have left the curricle somewhere, probably at a stable."

"At an inn," Dora interposed, wiping her eyes.

"Why an inn?"

"Clarisse hadn't had her lunch," Dora said simply.

"I will send William and George to make enquiries at all the inns on the outskirts of the main routes out of the city," said Tarquin as he left the room.

"When she reaches the convent will they make her a nun at once?" Simon asked.

"No indeed," Laurie was glad to reassure him. "It is three years before the final vows are taken."

"I had begun to fancy that she liked me a little," he said miserably and lapsed into a pensive silence interrupted by his elder brother's return.

"They will make extensive and discreet enquiry," Tarquin said.

"But we cannot merely wait here for information," Simon protested. "We must ride after them."

"As soon as we find out which road they have taken," Tarquin answered.

"Surely it will be the road by which we travelled?" said Laurie.

"If he has taken her to the convent at all," Tarquin said grimly.

"What do you imply?" Laurie stared at him.

"That David Cornwall is the last man to escort a young and attractive girl to a convent."

"That is a prejudiced remark," Simon retorted. "You have always disliked him."

"With good reason."

"You think he means to force her into wedlock?" Laurie asked.

"I think he means to force her, but not necessarily into wedlock."

"But that is dreadful!" Her face white, Laurie bit back a sob. "Clarisse is quite innocent."

"He may deceive her with a promise of marriage, and only use force if she rejects him."

"Which she most certainly will!"

"Or he may tell her they are taking another route to throw any pursuit off the scent. I cannot give you an exact forecast, save that he will not drive her to any convent."

"She will be ruined," Dora said, and began to weep, gently and becomingly as she did all things.

"I refuse to believe it," Simon declared, his voice shaking with indignation. "You have never liked my friends, Tarquin. Ever since you returned from the Americas you have looked down your nose at my acquaintances."

His voice trailed away as the other turned on his heel

and left. Laurie hesitated a moment, then followed him, but when she reached the side door he was already mounted and cantering out of the yard into the pouring rain.

There were occasions when Laurie could behave as impulsively as either of her younger sisters. This was such an occasion.

She ran to the stable and lifted down the sidesaddle. Rainbow whinnied eagerly as Laurie led her out of her stall and hastily saddled up. Then she was trotting through the yard and across the square just in time to catch a glimpse of Jasper's swishing tail as Tarquin rode down the alley. She had intended to follow at a distance, but Jasper sensed the presence of his stable companion and tossed his head.

"Where on earth do you think you are going?" Tarquin demanded, turning and checking his pace.

"I have to talk to you," Laurie said, ignoring the irritation in his tone.

"I will talk to you later at the house."

"Right now, if you please." She tried to fix him with a level look, but the rain made her blink.

"You will be soaked," he said impatiently.

"Then let us ride on. I will be less soaked than if we stay here," she retorted.

"Woman's logic," Tarquin said, but he rode on.

"Do you really believe that David Cornwall will try to seduce my sister?" Laurie asked.

"I am almost certain of it," he answered shortly.

"Why are you so certain?" The rain had eased a little, and she lifted her head to challenge him.

"Private reasons."

"Would they have anything to do with a girl who has a baby named after you?"

She had startled him. He jerked on the rein and swore softly under his breath.

"Why do you ask that?"

"I happened to see you with her." She chose her words

carefully, not wishing to involve her aunt. "You gave her money and she said that little Tarquin deserved a father."

"But that was in the tavern—but never mind. Yes, I gave her money. I do so from time to time. In gratitude for my help she named her son after me."

"But you are not the father."

"Of course not. Did you think I was?"

"At first, until it just dawned on me that the baby must have been conceived while you were in America and born after your return?"

"It is a pity," he said dryly, "that young ladies are not instructed more accurately about the facts of life."

"Is David Cornwall the father?" she asked bluntly.

"Yes." His reply was equally uncompromising.

"And the girl came to you for help?"

"She is not a cast-off mistress of my own," he said with a faint grin. "I am a friend of her brother."

"Her brother?"

"Ianto. Meg is Romany, and when a Romany girl bears a bastard child she is banished from the tribe. Ianto saved my life once. He helped me when I was set on by footpads years back, and we kept up the friendship. When I returned from America I looked for him in the usual camping ground. He told me about his sister's shame. I agreed to help her. That's all."

"Why doesn't David Cornwall support his own child?" Laurie asked indignantly.

"Meg refused to reveal the name of her lover to her family. She knew they would kill him, and she certainly had no wish to see members of her family hanged. She told me the truth under promise of secrecy, but that does not prevent me from disliking and distrusting the man. He has no morality, ho kindness."

"Surely the girl was also to blame," Laurie said, wanting to be fair.

"She told me that he forced her. I believe it," Tarquin said.

They were riding onto the heath. Taking notice of that,

Laurie said, "But now you are going to tell them?"

"Only that Clarisse has driven off with David Cornwall. The Romanies are the finest trackers I know. They will find the direction in which they have gone in half the time it would take the Bow Street Runners."

"You are not going to shame Clarisse by calling them in, are you?" she exclaimed.

"I am more likely to spank the wretched child," he retorted. "She might even benefit by a year or two in a convent, though I pity the community that takes her."

They were riding hard, though the rain-logged turf slowed their progress. Ahead of them thin, twisting columns of smoke rose from the camp fires. As they halted, a boy in ragged shirt and trousers, gold hoops in his ears, ran out of the thicket of trees, calling something in his own tongue. Tarquin dismounted, catching the lad by the shoulder and addressing him in the same language, spoken rather more slowly. The boy answered, his voice cracking with emotion, and Tarquin turned back to where Laurie sat in bewilderment on Rainbow.

"Petro says that Ianto is under arrest," he said. "The Runners came early this morning and arrested him on a charge of receiving stolen property. They are holding him at Bow Street Police Station. It's a hanging matter if he is found guilty. Apparently, he was found in possession of a diamond brooch, which sounds extraordinarily like the one my mother lost. I have told the boy to send trackers after the runaway pair, but I must go at once and see what I can do for Ianto."

The old woman had seen a hanging in Laurie's palm. The memory of that made her shiver. Her cousin looked at her with the first sign of concern he had shown. "You have caught a chill," he said. "You must ride home at once."

She shook her head obstinately. "I will ride with you. It is possible I may be able to throw light on this. Truly, Cousin, there is no point in arguing."

He gave her an exasperated look as he remounted. "I

begin to think there is no point in dealing with any of you as if you were civilised young ladies. Lord forbid that I should ever again be forced into guardianship of unreasonable females."

He had thrown his cloak about her as he spoke. Despite his manner, she sensed that he was more worried about his friend than angry with her. The rain, at least, was ceasing, but the darkness of early evening was closing down as well. They rode in silence, Laurie torn between two problems now—where Clarisse could be and how Aunt Marie's brooch had come into Ianto's possession.

"You look like a drowned rat," said Tarquin as they dismounted before the small, grim building. "I cannot imagine what you think you can contribute, but you had best come inside with me."

It was the least enthusiastic invitation she had ever received. At another time she might have smiled, but now she followed him meekly into a room furnished only with a desk, a couple of chairs, and several posters pinned up on the walls. At the desk sat a man in the dark blue of the Runners, a pipe in his mouth and a sheaf of papers before him.

"Tarquin St. John, and this is my cousin, Miss Laurentia St. John," Tarquin said briskly.

"How can I help you, sir?" The man at the desk recognised quality despite their bedraggled appearance.

"You are holding a man called Ianto Bohanna?"

"Gypsy. Accused of receiving stolen property by virtue of finding."

"There is a possibility that a grave error has been made," Tarquin said. "Was the brooch in the shape of a fern leaf, diamonds set in gold?"

"That it was." The man sat up straighter.

"My mother lost such a brooch," Tarquin said. "It is possible that Ianto picked it up as he says he did."

"Sorry, sir, but that's not likely." The other drew on his pipe and shook his head. "We have a witness ready to swear that the brooch is his and that the Gypsy jostled him and snatched it."

"What witness?" Laurie broke in.

"French gentleman, name of Delmain. Says he was taking the brooch to have the clasp mended when the Gypsy grabbed it from his hand. There's no brooch like it been reported missing or stolen, so we have to take Mr. Delmain's word that the brooch is his property."

"What would a man be doing with a diamond brooch?" Laurie demanded.

"Thinking of giving it to a lady," the other said. "I don't trust Frenchies myself, but it seems feasible—them all being inordinately fond of the ladies. Not that I'd fancy my daughter marrying one. I never could abide a man who wore a ring with stones in it."

"A ruby ring?"

"Yes, miss. Very large and vulgar." He gave her an inquisitive look. "Do you know the man, miss?"

"Not actually," she said lamely, avoiding her cousin's gaze.

She could say nothing until she had talked to Aunt Marie and found out the truth, which she wondered if her aunt would be willing to tell.

"I'd like to talk to Ianto Bohanna," Tarquin said. "I take it he's been charged?"

"He goes before the magistrate in the morning," the Runner told him.

"He has a lawyer? I will undertake to pay for legal advice."

"Said he didn't need one," the other said. "Said as how he was innocent and lawyers were all twisted. I'm inclined to agree, though it don't do to say. This way and mind the step."

The staircase and passage below were dimly lit and smelt of damp, cold, and something else that Laurie sensed to be fear. There were barred cells on both sides of the passage. She walked nervously down the middle until they reached the end. In the dim light it was possible to make out the figure of the Romany, seated disconsolately on a bunk, the faint light reflecting from the rings in his ears.

"Tarquin!" He was on his feet in an instant, and they gripped hands through the bars. "You went to the camp."

"On other business. What is this nonsense of finding a diamond brooch?"

"I found it on the Frenchie," Ianto replied with a faint grin. "He wasn't about to have it mended either. He was trying to sell it. He had been offered a price he reckoned was too low in one shop and he was on his way to another. He was turning the brooch over in his hand when I took it. I've seen your mother driving out with that very same brooch pinned to her dress, and I didn't think there'd be two like it in London. That is why I took it."

"But why not voice your suspicions as to the real owner?" Tarquin asked, perplexed.

"I don't trust the magistrates to pay attention to a Gypsy. I reckoned that you'd turn up sooner or later and explain everything."

"You have a touching faith in my being in the right place at the right time," said Tarquin. "I'll go and see what Mama has to say at once. She can confirm the brooch is hers, and then it will be the Frenchman who will have some explaining to do."

"Don't be too long about it then," Ianto said cheerfully. "I can't abide this place for more than a night."

Laurie could not have abided it for so long. She nodded silently to the Romany and experienced infinite relief as they mounted the stairs again.

"The brooch is here, sir," the Runner informed them. "I can't let it out of my sight since it's evidence, but if your mother can come down here early tomorrow and swear that it belongs to her with something to confirm that, then we can talk to Mr. Delmain again and find out the truth of the matter."

"I will see to it," Tarquin promised, bringing out a pile of coins. "See the men in the cells get a decent supper tonight, won't you?"

"Indeed I will, sir."

"And have a good supper yourself." Tarquin added more coins as they were bowed out into a rain-glistened street with the lamps already making pools of honey on the wet road.

"I shall have a word with Mr. Delmain myself as soon as the opportunity arises," Tarquin said as he helped her to mount. "And you can explain later how you come to have any knowledge of the fellow's jewellery. For now, let's get back and find out if anything has been discovered of the runaways. You will keep what I told you about David Cornwall to yourself. I have neither liking nor approval for the man, but to seduce a girl, even when it is without her consent, is not a murdering matter. I would not lay that crime upon my friends."

Laurie inclined her head and was relieved when he turned in the direction of home and abstained from further conversation. Dinner was being served when they reached the house, though there were only Aunt Marie and Dora at the long table. Laurie rushed upstairs to change into dry garments and towel the dampness out of her hair. Upon entering the dining room, she was greeted by Dora with a warm embrace.

"'I thought that you and Tarquin had eloped too."

"Clarisse hasn't eloped," Laurie said, irritated. "She imagines she is on her way to a convent."

"I have been praying that Cousin Tarquin has misjudged Mr. Cornwall, and that he will really take her there," said Dora fervently, resuming her seat.

"Simon rode out onto the Great North Road," Aunt Marie said. "He begins to think they are bound for Gretna Green. I have never been so fretted in my entire life. Laurentia, where have you been?"

"Helping me to locate your missing brooch, Mama," Tarquin said.

"Brooch?" Aunt Marie was eating soup, and now she set the spoon down very carefully.

"The diamond and gold fern-leaf brooch that Papa gave you. You told Simon that it was lost. I wish that you had told me also, or did you imagine that I would scold you for carelessness?"

"The brooch was not actually lost," Aunt Marie said. She had picked up her spoon again and was stirring it round and round in the bowl.

"But you told Simon it was! Mama, a friend of mine, Ianto Bohanna, from the Romany camp has been accused of stealing it from a Frenchman called Delmain. You recall Ianto?"

"He came to help out when one of the horses was spavined. He is not a gentleman."

"More of a gentleman than some," Tarquin said curtly. "If your brooch was not lost, then what did happen to it?"

"I think you forget that you are speaking to your mother," she began.

"No, and I do not forget that my friend is accused of stealing your brooch and will hang unless he can prove that he was merely trying to return it to you."

"I sold the brooch," Aunt Marie said after a long moment.

"You sold the brooch that Papa gave you?" Tarquin was staring at her.

"Sold it," Aunt Marie said flatly.

"Why? You cannot possibly need the money."

"The truth is," said Aunt Marie, beginning to speak very rapidly, "the truth is that I have been somewhat careless about investments and—well, my losses at cards have been greater than I expected."

"Mama, your losses at cards would scarcely justify your selling a hat pin." Tarquin said impatiently. "If you found yourself temporarily embarrassed for funds you could easily have drawn on the bank. What made you think that you needed to sell Papa's brooch? It was a favourite piece of yours."

"I refuse to be questioned as if I were in a witness stand," Aunt Marie said. "I have a perfect right to dispose of my property as I choose, and I will not discuss the matter further."

"I do wish that we knew what was happening about Clarisse," Dora said suddenly. "It is worrying me dreadfully."

That Dora was worried showed the situation to be serious.

"William and George brought back information that a gentleman answering Mr. Cornwall's description had stopped to hire a post chaise at a hostelry on the Great North Road." There was faint relief in Aunt Marie's voice as she said this. No doubt she was glad to have the subject diverted from her own affairs.

"Then he does plan to force her into wedlock." Laurie felt a wave of depression.

"Unless he is taking a detour to avoid pursuit?" Dora said brightly.

"To travel southwest by way of the Great North Road would be a detour indeed," Tarquin commented. "However, as Simon has ridden after them, we may be sure that he will find them. My brother may have his faults, but when he makes up his mind to something he carries it through. Mama, if you choose to dispose of your jewellery, that is your right, but in my opinion it is completely unnecessary. I suggest we finish our meal and then I must seek a lawyer. Ianto will be in need of the best I can find."

But it ought not to be so, Laurie thought, dutifully chewing her dinner without tasting one morsel of it. Her aunt was lying. She had not sold the brooch but had given it to the Frenchman, and Ianto had recognised it and wrested it back from the man. Unless her aunt told the truth, Tarquin's friend would probably hang. She wondered if a personal appeal to the older woman might serve, but decided it would not. Aunt Marie had only agreed to sponsor her nieces out of a belated sense of duty, and though her initial frostiness had warmed, she was unlikely to respond to any plea that Laurie might advance.

The only course of action to take was so simple and so audacious that for an instant Laurie caught her breath. The Frenchman must be forced to relinquish whatever he had that her aunt was paying to keep hidden. There had to be some way of getting into his room. Meanwhile, desserts were being brought in.

She cast an apologetic look at the others and murmured, "May I be excused? I have such a headache after all the events of the day."

"I think I will go and practise," Dora announced. "Would it disturb you, Laurie? I will play very softly. I can soothe my own fears at the pianoforte."

"I will probably be sound asleep in moments," Laurie said mendaciously, then added, "It is not that I am not concerned about Clarisse, but if Simon has gone after them, I am sure he will bring her back safely."

Laurie left the room, trying to convey by a drooping gait that her head was filled with pain instead of plans.

== 13 ==

GETTING INTO SIMON'S room was easy, as was gathering what garments she would need from his wardrobe. Fitting herself into the clothes had proved rather more difficult since though she was slender and fairly tall, Laurie and her cousin were certainly not the same shape. However, by dint of holding her breath, she squeezed herself into his skintight breeches and turned up the overlong sleeves of the shirt under the coat. Unfortunately, there was no way of emulating his elegantly tied cravats. She had to content herself with a simple bow and pulled on her own riding boots.

Her hair was another difficulty. In the end she looped it and tied it back in a pigtail, cramming his hat on top and trusting that she might be taken for a nautical gentleman. She had been disappointed to see an empty pistol case by his bed, but there was another pistol hanging on the wall over the fireplace. She took that down gingerly and tucked it into her belt under the skirts of the coat.

Getting out of the house by way of the side door and saddling up Rainbow also proved unexpectedly easy. Tarquin must have ridden out, since Jasper's stall was vacant, and the grooms were nowhere in sight. Most likely, they were enjoying a supper in the kitchen and gossiping about Clarisse's flight.

Laurie saddled Rainbow and led her out of the yard. The long curtains at the front windows were drawn so

Laurie was able to use the front steps as a mounting block. She had ridden astride before and secretly preferred it, though the unaccustomed freedom of legs encased in breeches instead of being hampered by a long, narrow skirt took some adjusting to. She gathered up the reins, sparing only a moment to send up a small prayer of gratitude that the rain hadn't started again, and trotted out of the square.

It was not yet nine and the streets were still full of traffic and pedestrians. She was glad of her excellent sense of direction as she rode towards the gallery where they had gone to look at the exhibition. The street where the Frenchman lodged was behind it. It was not a long ride, and she was further cheered by the fact that in her progress not a single person turned to look at her. A solitary youth riding through the city called for no particular attention.

The crowds thinned as she left the main road and wended her way past the tavern where she had seen Tarquin meeting Meg. A faint blush mantled her cheeks as she recalled how she had misjudged him. There was no bar in the way of his falling in love with Dora now, she reflected, and sighed despite herself.

She had not worked out exactly how she would gain entrance to Delmain's lodging, but again luck was with her. As she dismounted, the door of the house opened and a slatternly looking woman appeared on the threshold.

"If it's the Frenchie you aim to see, he just stepped out for a breath of air. He said as how his lawyer might call round, and if so I was to send you up. Third on left. Door's not locked. You can leave your horse in the yard for threepence."

The yard was at the back of the building and fortunately dimly lit. Laurie tethered Rainbow under the makeshift shelter and gave the woman the coins, judging rightly that the clink of money would distract her from peering too closely at the visitor's face. The staircase was rickety.

Laurie mounted with care and pushed open the third door at the left. The room was dingy, furnished with a high bed, a table, and a chair. There was a lamp burning which suggested that the occupier intended to return soon.

Laurie stood uncertainly in the middle of the floor, wondering where to start searching, and not in the least certain what she was seeking. Whatever the man had that could be used to frighten Aunt Marie into giving him her diamond brooch, he probably kept on his person, unless he thought it wiser left in a safe hiding place lest his victim find the courage to have him attacked and robbed.

The floor creaked under her feet as she shifted her weight. An instant later she was rolling back the strip of thin carpet and lifting up the board beneath. It concealed a flat parcel, thin enough to fit easily into the confined space and protected by a wrapping of oilskin. Laurie took it out and laid it on the table, hoping she hadn't stumbled inadvertently on the landlady's last will and testament or something equally innocuous. The document was only faintly yellowed, the clerkly black script in French. She read slowly, trying to still the beating of her heart.

Her French, despite Miss Browne's efforts, was not fluent, but there was no mistaking the import of what she read. In the Year of Our Lord Seventeen Hundred and Eighty-Eight, Marie Claire, Aged Seventeen, of the Rue St. Germain, Paris, had married Alphonse Delmain, Aged Eighteen, of Montmartre, Paris.

On the eve of the revolution that had destroyed her family, Aunt Marie had taken a husband. Perhaps the marriage had been an arranged one. Perhaps it had been unhappy. Whatever the circumstances, Marie Delmain nee Claire had married an Englishman the following year and sailed to England, her family already under arrest.

Laurie heard the door open and spun round, pulling the pistol from her belt and levelling it with both hands.

"Don't try firing that thing," Tarquin advised. "It hasn't been loaded for years."

"You went to see your lawyer," she said in disbelief.

"And you went to bed with a headache, if I remember correctly. We do seem to keep on running into one another in the most out-of-the-way places. I got the Address of Monsieur Delmain's lodging at the Bow Street Station and rode here in the hope of persuading him to drop the charges. What's this?"

Before she could prevent him he had stepped to the table and picked up the document. His face hardened slightly as he read it, but he made no comment till he'd completed a second perusal.

"You have seen this?" he asked.

She nodded.

"Mama was trying to buy his silence." His voice was thoughtful. "I always felt there were certain things in her past that she wished to keep hidden. I doubt if my father knew."

"It needn't make any difference," she said breathlessly. "We can destroy the document, and nobody will ever know."

"My dear cousin, it makes a great deal of difference. If this is genuine, and I am sure that it is, then Mama wed Papa when her first husband was still living, which makes their union invalid and my brother and I illegitimate."

"Oh dear!" Laurie sat down abruptly on the only chair.

"Oh dear indeed," Tarquin echoed. "I won't enquire how you came to be here. I am of the opinion that if I had business in the South Seas I would find you there before me. . . . Hush!"

They had both heard the step outside the door. Tarquin's pistol was in his hand smooth as silk when Delmain entered. The Frenchman's eyes fell first on Laurie, then he swung round to find himself confronting a forearm.

"I assume you speak English?" Tarquin sounded as polite as if they had just dropped by for tea.

"Fluently," Delmain said.

Laurie was forced to admire the speed with which he had summed up the situation, and the coolness of his reply.

"Blackmail is a very serious crime," her cousin said in a conversational tone.

"So is bigamy," Delmain said.

"And so is attempted rape," Laurie put in.

"Rape! What is he—she talking about?" the Frenchman demanded.

"You don't recall the young lady you accosted in the park? You had been watching my aunt's house, I daresay," Laurie said. "On the evening we arrived, Tarquin. I didn't wish to cause a pother, but this man tried to attack me in the park. I recognised the ruby ring. I am quite willing to give evidence against him."

"It wouldn't stand up in court," the Frenchman sneered.

"When your blackmailing activities are fully investigated," Tarquin said, "other charges would be believed more easily. Are you willing to take the risk?"

"I thought Marie was dead along with the rest of her family," Delmain muttered. "I fell on hard times. When I came to England I hoped to better myself. I took employment that was not fit for a gentleman and never troubled her, not even when I discovered she was still alive."

"You waited until my father died before you moved in, isn't that it? You would not go up against another man. But a woman was a different matter."

"My lawyer's coming round to advise me on my evidence against the Gypsy," Delmain said. "I can bring charges against you too—for intimidation."

"And the marriage certificate can also be produced in court," Tarquin pointed out. Delmain glowered, but it was clear that he was yielding. He chewed his lower lip for a moment.

"What is it you want?" he asked finally.

"You have pen and ink and paper?"

"On the shelf," he said.

"Get them, Laurie. Now, Monsieur Delmain, you will write a brief statement declaring that having learned your wife, whom you believed dead, had remarried, also believing you to be dead, you set out to blackmail her into buying your silence."

The Frenchman lowered his bulk onto the chair from which Laurie had risen and began to write.

"Now add that Ianto Bohanna, recognising the brooch in your possession, tried to wrest it away from you with the intention of returning it to its rightful owner, but you laid false charges against him."

There was no sound in the room now but the scratching of the pen.

"Add that you also made improper advances to Miss Laurentia St. John when you accosted her in the park," Tarquin finished. "Then sign it neatly, sand it, and pass it to me."

"You ask a lot," Delmain said, but he continued to write.

"Keep this safe, Laurie." Tarquin took the completed paper and gave it, together with the marriage certificate, into her hands. "Delmain, when your lawyer arrives you will tell him you made a gross error of judgement. Then you will go straight to Bow Street to withdraw your charges against Ianto Bohanna. I want him freed as quickly as possible, and I want you on a ship bound for some foreign port by tomorrow night."

Laurie opened her mouth to protest that he was getting off lightly but closed it again as her cousin's eye fell on her.

"That's it then?" Delmain's tone conveyed his opinion that he too thought he was getting off lightly.

"That's all," Tarquin said. "Ah, the doorbell is ringing. I daresay that is your lawyer. Be sure to withdraw those charges. Laurie, put that weapon away. We don't want to throw a scare into the landlady."

They descended the stairs in silence and went round to the yard where Jasper and his stable companion were tethered side by side.

"You guessed that I was here!" Laurie said.

"When I saw Rainbow. Dora is far too much of a lady to go riding about after dark without escort."

"Oh." Somewhat crushed, Laurie mounted Rainbow.

"Do you think Delmain will do as he promised?" she ventured as they rode into the street.

"He has no choice. That seedy-looking fellow we passed as we came out is not going to risk any trouble with a criminal client. Now we'll head for home unless you have some other unfinished business. You were not considering taking up highway robbery by any chance?"

"You don't have to be sarcastic," Laurie said coldly and rode on ahead.

"My mother is very likely retired for the night," Tarquin remarked as they came through the side door. He was proved wrong by the sound of Aunt Marie's voice from the drawing room upstairs.

"Tarquin, will you come here? I have something of the utmost importance to say to you."

Tarquin glanced at Laurie, and by tacit consent they went up the stairs together. Aunt Marie sat bolt upright in a high-backed chair by the fireplace. Her face was very pale, her mouth set tightly with determination and what might be remembered pain. For the first time in Laurie's memory, her aunt looked every day of her age.

"I cannot justify it to my conscience—Laurentia, what on earth?" Her haggard gaze had fallen on her niece.

"Aunt Marie, Tarquin and I can guess what you intend to say," Laurie said swiftly. "I do beg you to believe that it makes no difference."

"How can you possibly know?" Her aunt broke off, staring at the paper Laurie had put into her hands.

"You can destroy it," Laurie said urgently. "Nobody need ever know."

"My quixotic cousin," Tarquin murmured. "My dear girl, there will be other records of the marriage upon which future generations may well stumble, causing the most unearthly family row. The marriage itself can be quietly dissolved without any of Mama's friends even being aware of it, and of course Gables will now revert to you, the entail not applying to—sons in our position."

"It was an arranged marriage," Aunt Marie said. Her hands were so tightly clasped that the knuckles showed white. "He was unpleasant even when he was a boy. Then my parents were called in for questioning. On the eve of the Revolution there was great unease, many arrests. Alphonse ordered me to make for the coast. Your father was returning to England after a business trip to the Continent. He was very kind to me. I told him I was unmarried, travelling to find a position in England. He offered his escort and we were married a few months later. Then I heard my relatives had been guillotined and I assumed that Alphonse was dead too."

"He assumed that you were dead as well, until he came to England and found out you had remarried. He waited until Papa was dead before he made himself known to you," Tarquin said.

"I gave him the diamond brooch in return for his promise of silence. It was the worst luck in the world that the Gypsy should run into him and recognise it as being mine."

"Or the best luck," Tarquin said. "You won't be troubled by Alphonse Delmain again. He was obliging enough to write this for me. With that as evidence, you can obtain your divorce in your maiden name without many questions. It will be the end of the matter, and Gables can be quietly handed over to Laurie as a gift if she will agree. For myself I don't mind, but Simon's future could be clouded by these revelations."

"I don't want Gables," Laurie said.

"For a girl who has clearly been pining for her childhood home ever since she set foot in London that's an extraordinarily foolish remark," Tarquin said. "If you have any scruples about depriving me of the place you can discard them. I have money of my own, and Gables is something of a white elephant, judging from the bills for the renovations that are now arriving."

"We will, of course, pay back every penny," said Laurie stiffly.

"Otherwise, I shall certainly throw you into debtors' prison." He touched her lightly on the shoulder. "It's near midnight, Cousin. Go to bed. Dora will be in dreamland already."

"What about Clarisse?" she lingered to say.

"If Simon has caught up with them—and I have every confidence in my brother's horsemanship—then Clarisse will be on her way home by now. I will sit up for them myself if you insist."

"No, I—I am sure they will be all right." Laurie glanced towards her aunt and added uncertainly, "I do beg you not to distress yourself about all this, ma'am. Nobody else need ever be told anything."

"I never invited you to stay or visited you when your father was alive because I could not endure to be reminded that you would lose your home to an entail by which my sons had no legal right to benefit," Aunt Marie said and gave a harsh, dry sob.

"You have been the soul of hospitality," Laurie said warmly. "We are most grateful to you."

"And you will remain here for the Season." Tarquin spoke as he accompanied her from the room.

"If you wish it, Cousin."

"For my own part I shall be quite relieved when the house is quiet again," he said, "but Dora appears to be making a social stir, and I have the impression that Simon will welcome the opportunity to further his friendship with Clarisse."

"She is very set on entering a convent," Laurie warned.

"An ambition I shall continue to do my best to discourage," he countered.

"Does that mean you still consider yourself to be our guardian?" she asked sharply.

"In the strictly legal sense I suppose that I am not," he admitted. "However, as the circumstances of my mother's first marriage are to be kept private, I would regard it as a favour if we continued to observe the proprieties."

"You may call yourself guardian," Laurie said, "as long as you don't try to stop us doing what we wish."

"A truly alarming prospect!" He looked down at her for a long moment, then tilted her chin abruptly and kissed her lips. "Go and take off those borrowed breeches," he ordered, "and try to sleep. I have no doubt that Simon will bring Clarisse back unharmed."

He strode back down the passage, leaving her to stare at his retreating back. It was useless to try to sleep after that. She changed direction when she was halfway to Simon's room and veered into the music room instead. The lamps still burned, and there were sheets of music scattered on the top of the pianoforte with notations in Dora's spidery hand. Laurie brushed her fingers lightly across the silent keys. Words rose unbidden in her mind. She hunted for quill and ink to capture those words before they fled.

It was as if the emotions churning within her had forced themselves onto the paper, demanding life. She settled herself at the small desk in the corner. The outside world dimmed as her inner world expressed itself.

Once there was a heart. Stolen now.
No need to cry.
Once there was a man. I saw his face,
Passing by.
World full of people, streets wet with rain,
When will I find that sweet thief again,
Holding my heart in his hands?
Once there was a heart. Stolen now.
No need to cry.
Once there was a man. I felt his kiss,
Passing by.
World full of people, streets bright with sun,
When will he know the harm he has done,
Holding my heart in his hands?

It required polishing but, for the moment, would have

to serve. She rose and left the music room, suddenly aching in every bone.

In her cousin's room she retrieved her own clothes and sat down wearily on the edge of his bed. Gables was her own again, though her sisters and Simon must always believe that it was a gift. It wasn't likely that Simon would object to his elder brother's generous gesture. When the Season was over she could go home again. She jumped up as an agitated ringing at the front door bell brought footsteps and voices.

"Clarisse!" The exclamation came from Dora, who appeared hurriedly pulling on a dressing gown.

She and Laurie almost collided at the head of the stairs, as Tarquin opened the door, and Aunt Marie emerged from the drawing room.

It was Clarisse all right, her red hair standing up wildly in all directions, her words tumbling over one another. "He will kill him. Simon will kill him or the other way round, which will be just as bad. For Mr. Cornwall will likely hang or have to flee the country. I was quite unhurt, only most indignant at being deceived, but Simon wouldn't listen. Five o'clock on the heath, he said, and rushed off to find seconds. Someone has to stop them, for it's against the law and Mr. Cornwall was quite ready to apologise."

"What is happening now?" Aunt Marie rustled forward.

"As far as I can gather," Tarquin answered calmly, "Clarisse has come back, and Simon is to fight a duel with David Cornwall at five o'clock on Hampstead Heath."

"That's against the law, isn't it?" Dora enquired, yawning.

"Indeed it is," Tarquin assured her. "Mama, there is no need to faint or weep. It is still four hours short of five o'clock. Where did my brother say he was going to find his seconds?"

"He didn't." Clarisse had stepped inside, her gaze seeking her sisters. "He just went off, and Mr. Cornwall went off as well, in the other direction. Then the coachman brought me home. Why is Laurie wearing breeches?"

"She went riding astride," Tarquin said.

"I thought you went to bed with a headache," Dora commented reproachfully. "I purposely didn't play loudly."

"I daresay she went looking for me," Clarisse said, not without a certain complacency.

"I had other things on my mind." Laurie descended the stairs and frowned at her sister. "I am, however, exceedingly shocked at your behaviour, Clarisse. I never dreamed you could be so underhand."

"I was sorry about it almost as soon as we started out," Clarisse confessed. "Mr. Cornwall acted in the most peculiar fashion, insisting we were on the right road when I knew we were going north instead of south, then trying to persuade me to continue on to Gretna Green. He had actually reserved only one room at the coaching inn, and I was very cross and very pleased when Simon rode up. I felt just like a heroine in a tale. I don't suppose I could have something to eat, could I? It is simply ages since we had supper, and they were awfully stingy about second helpings."

== 14 ==

SOMEWHERE IN THE house the grandfather clock chimed four. Laurie, coat and boots off now, woke from a brief doze and forced herself to sit up in the big armchair where she had curled herself. She had decided against lying down on the bed for fear she should fall into a heavy sleep and so miss the duel—or rather the nonduel—since she was quite determined to do something to prevent it. Whatever the right or wrong of the matter, it was unthinkable that Simon and David Cornwall should be allowed to fire at each other in defiance of the law. If anything happened to either of them, Clarisse would never forgive herself. Her agitation had been all for Simon, which boded well for their future relationship, but Clarisse would most definitely flee into a convent if anything serious occurred as a result of her escapade.

Upon her return, she had been given supper, fetched by a sleepy and inquisitive Jane, and a scolding to flavour it from Laurie, who welcomed the opportunity to release some of her pent-up feelings.

"To deceive us all was very wrong. What did you propose to tell the Sisters when you got to St. Cecilia's? That you were seeking sanctuary or something equally fantastical, I daresay. Don't you think they would have checked immediately to find out if you had permission to enter? They seldom take girls under the age of eighteen anyway unless they have a very strong vocation. I doubt if a girl who tells lies and feigns a sprained ankle would be considered a very suitable candidate."

"I really am sorry," Clarisse said. "Mr. Cornwall made it sound the right thing to do. He agreed that it would save Aunt the expense of my coming out when I had no intention of every marrying. It was only later that he began to talk in a most ungentlemanly way. I never saw anybody change so rapidly."

"I have no doubt my brother's eyes have been opened," Tarquin remarked.

"Oh, Simon was absolutely splendid," Clarisse said. "He called Mr. Cornwall a puppy and a besmircher of females."

"Clary!" her sisters exclaimed in unison.

"I merely repeat," Clarisse said with dignity. "It was not really accurate, since I had not been besmirched, but it sounded very fierce. I am only afraid that Mr. Cornwall will turn out a crack shot and injure Simon."

"Do be quiet or Aunt will overhear you," Laurie begged.

Aunt Marie had finally been persuaded to retire with the promise that the duel would be stopped before a shot was fired, but Laurie had sensed a certain reservation in her cousin's tone that made her suspect he was telling less than the truth.

"Did they mention where exactly on the heath this meeting was to take place?" Tarquin was asking.

Clarisse took another bite of her plum tart before she answered. "Near Hangman's Oak. Do you know it?"

"A conventional duelling spot."

"Is Simon a good shot?" Laurie enquired.

"Middling fair. I would not have let him ride off to intercept the coach had I realised it might actually come to a challenge. I had envisaged something more in the nature of a fistfight."

"He threatened that too," Clarisse said. "You don't think Simon will really be wounded? I would dislike that above all things."

"I cannot imagine why," her cousin said equably. "A nun is supposed to be detached from worldly affection, is she not?"

"I am not actually a nun yet," Clarisse reminded him.

"But you have shown us all how intense your longing to enter a convent is," he replied. "I believe I was wrong to forbid you before. I didn't take you seriously and I apologise for that. When this business is over we must reconsider the question."

"Oh," said Clarisse.

"I think we ought to go back to bed," Dora suggested. "It won't help Simon if we sit up all night. Cousin Tarquin will prevent the duel."

Nothing upset Dora for long, Laurie thought, watching her sister drift from the room. Clarisse, whose appetite seemed to have fled for once, murmured a subdued good night and followed.

"I believe she will be rather less eager to run into a convent once she knows that I have no objection to the idea," Tarquin mused. "You were right, Laurie. I handled that affair very badly."

"And the duel?"

The smile vanished from his lips. "David Cornwall is a crack shot. I cannot possibly allow Simon to go through with this nonsense."

"He is of age," she reminded him. "Will he listen to you?"

"I'm hoping so. Go to bed, Laurie. This has been a long day for you."

His voice and eyes were so kind and concerned that she longed to move nearer, to seek the circle of his arms, but she nodded instead and left the room.

Now the chiming of the clock reminded her that the day wasn't over yet. In an hour Simon and David Cornwall would fight at Hangman's Oak.

The house was in moonlit silence as she let herself out by the side door. The grooms would be asleep. She drew a breath of relief as she saw that the stable was latched but not locked. In this quiet square, robbery was almost unknown. She saddled up Rainbow quickly and quietly, noting that Jasper was gone. Tarquin had already ridden out.

She felt the pull of the unloaded pistol at her belt as she mounted and decided that if she were accosted she could always flourish it. However, that proved unnecessary. The streets were empty, and she reached the outskirts of the heath without incident. The undulating turf with its clumps of brambles and bracken was washed silver by the moon and the few trees stood silent sentinel.

Where was Hangman's Oak? She had not dared to make enquiry as to its exact location lest Tarquin guess her intention, though that might be crediting him with the gift of clairvoyance since Laurie had no clear intention at all. She only knew that she was incapable of lying peacefully in her bed while her cousins could be engaged in violent struggle.

Horses were approaching from the left. She glimpsed black silhouettes in the moon glow. Then they vanished behind a grove of trees. It was unlikely there would be more than one group of riders on the heath at this hour. She dismounted, walking forward cautiously over the tussocks of pale grass.

The oak tree that spread its branches over a circle of toadstools had a weird and twisted aspect in this light, though by day it probably turned itself into an ordinary tree again. The riders had dismounted and were tethering their horses. She heard Tarquin's voice.

"This is a madcap scheme. Clarisse was not harmed."

"But would have been had I not arrived," Simon's belligerent tone answered.

"Cornwall is an excellent shot and may wound you severely."

"Or I may wound him."

"And both of you are breaking the law."

"That is the least of my problems," her younger cousin

said.

Another voice spoke. Laurie recognised it as belonging to a young man with whom she had danced. James someone or other.

"At least we have an excellent physician," he said.

"A mixed blessing, if you'll pardon my saying so," Tarquin snapped. "Were you not here, doctor, the two young hotheads might think twice before blazing away at each other."

"You always talk as if you were fifty years old instead of not yet thirty," Simon said irritably. "You have sown your own wild oats and refuse to allow anyone else to do the same."

"Sow as many wild oats as you please but don't get killed in the process." Tarquin suddenly cocked his head and listened. "Who's there?" His tone sharpened as he swung round.

Laurie stepped out from the screen of high bushes where she stood. As if on cue the first light of dawn streaked the sky and the moon paled.

"Cousin Laurie." There was resignation but little surprise in Tarquin's voice. "I might have known you would not stay quietly in your bed. The stable door was unlocked, I suppose, and you decided to give Rainbow some exercise."

"I came to prevent the duel," Laurie said. "Simon, it is quite ridiculous for you to fight. If you are killed or wounded, then Clarisse will most certainly flee into a convent and your rescuing her will have been for nothing."

"Did you think that I would not advance the selfsame argument?" Tarquin enquired.

"I thought you might offer to fight in his stead," she confessed.

"It would certainly be a more even contest," he agreed, "but I allow my brother to fight his own battles if I cannot persuade him to take a more rational course. I cannot imagine what you hoped to achieve by coming."

His tone stung her. He sounded as if she had acted like a romantical fool, she thought, with nothing in her head. That Laurie herself was inclined to concur with that estimate of herself only made her more furious.

"We should not have agreed to leave Gables at all," she burst out in exasperation.

"Cousin, I am inclined to agree—Here comes Cornwall with his seconds!"

The heath was getting quite crowded, Laurie thought, as dawn revealed the approaching trio, mounted and wearing heavy cloaks.

"What the devil is Miss St. John doing here?" was David Cornwall's first remark.

"Hoping to prevent an unlawful and unnecessary duel," Laurie flashed. "It was my sister whom you tried to lure away, so if anyone were to kill you—and you thoroughly deserve it—my family would be very embarrassed by it. Otherwise, I would urge Simon to shoot you immediately."

"Your cousin is wonderfully fierce," David said. "Are you of the same strong stomach, St. John?"

"I thought you my friend," Simon said hotly. "You are no friend and no gentleman."

"It was funning. I will not apologise for a practical joke. I would not have harmed the girl."

"Will you apologise?" Tarquin demanded.

"Your brother called me out. To apologise would be to admit myself a coward."

"Or a man of honour. You are known as a crack shot."

"I don't intend to shoot to kill," David Cornwall said.

"I do!" Simon said loudly.

"Let us be done with all this nonsense," Laurie cried in despair. "You played a very scurvy trick on Clarisse, Mr. Cornwall. I believed you to be a respectable young man, but you are a scoundrel—and not only in the way you sought to run off with my sister!" She broke off, seeing Tarquin's warning look. He had told her to keep silent about Meg who had borne Cornwall's child. If the Bohannas found out about it they would certainly hunt down her seducer, and then there would be the hanging that Mama Sarah had foretold.

"Do you wish to withdraw your challenge?" David Cornwall asked Simon.

"I do not." Her cousin's expression was mulish.

"Then I suggest we proceed. It is almost full light." David Cornwall began to strip off his cloak, beckoning one of his friends to approach with the case of weapons he carried.

"Pistols? It is for me to choose the weapon, I believe?" David Cornwall spoke politely.

This was utterly stupid and completely unrealistic, Laurie thought. David Cornwall was an unpleasant young man who needed a horsewhipping instead of the opportunity to pink her hotheaded cousin. Without making excuses for Mr. Cornwall's behaviour, she was forced to admit that Clarisse had encouraged him by her disobedience.

Tarquin stepped aside, apparently unwilling to hurt his brother's pride by arguing with him further. The two duellists chose their pistols, and the doctor, looking acutely ill at ease, produced a black bag from which he ostentatiously brought forth bandages and what looked like a flask of brandy.

It was becoming more certain by the minute that someone might get very badly hurt here. Laurie's temper flared so suddenly that she startled even herself as she jerked the old pistol out of her belt and ran forward. She had it in her mind that David Cornwall wouldn't realise the pistol wasn't loaded and would back down. Instead, her foot slipped on the dew-damp grass, and the weapon, pointed waveringly in David Cornwall's general direction, went off. The recoil sent a jarring pain up her arm. When the smoke cleared, she found herself lying flat on her stomach with the wind knocked out of her, while at a little distance, David Cornwall clutched his shoulder, groaning.

"By Jove, you shot him!" Simon cried.

"The pistol wasn't loaded," Laurie said, sitting up.

"Loaded it myself a couple of months back," Simon said. "I'd a fancy to try it out, but something or other came up and I stuck it back on the wall."

"Careless." Tarquin stepped forward and hauled Laurie, none too gently, to her feet. "It looks as if you are cheated of your duel today. Your erstwhile friend is in no state to fire a gun."

"Flesh wound." The doctor spoke brightly, as if the sight of blood had cheered him.

"Attempted murder!" David Cornwall glared at them.

"An unfortunate accident," Tarquin said. "I think we are all ready to bear witness to my cousin's having slipped when the apparently unloaded gun discharged itself."

"Wouldn't do to have a young lady arraigned for murder," said James something or other.

"You'd better accept Mr. Cornwall's apology, Simon," Tarquin said. "He will be willing to make a handsome one, I'll be bound, and to refrain from encouraging you to lose all your allowance on horses whose jockeys are in his employ."

"How did you find that out?" David Cornwall looked up from the tussock on which he was seated, undergoing the ministrations of the doctor.

"I may not be in the habit of firing off pistols or challenging people to duels," answered Tarquin, "but I do make it my business to keep informed. I'd advise a long period in some other part of the country for your convalescence."

"I've a mind to call you out all over again," Simon cried.

"Simon, we have all of us had a long hard night," his brother said wearily. "May I suggest that we part company for a few hours. Mr. Cornwall has a journey to arrange, and you will no doubt wish to take breakfast with your seconds before coming home to assure your cousin that you were ready to die for her but were not given the opportunity."

Laurie stood unsteadily and drew the morning air deep into her lungs. The prospect of almost killing a man was so unpleasant that she sensibly decided to postpone thinking about it until later.

"If you have no other pressing business, Cousin Laurentia, perhaps I may escort you home?" Tarquin was saying.

She inclined her head with what dignity she could muster and allowed him to lift her to the saddle. The other riders were remounting as well, to depart in their separate directions. Rainbow and Jasper, doubtless hoping for some uninterrupted rest free from the whims of human beings, trotted docilely towards the main road.

"I am thinking of paying a trip to the Americas," Tarquin said. "I have a ranch there, you know, in the hands of an excellent manager but I shall check on it myself. To tell you the truth, the conventions of polite society begin to bore me a little. Ever since I returned, I have been trying to take my late father's place, to fill his shoes. I begin to see that it is better for people to make their own mistakes as I was allowed to do."

"We shall miss you," was all that Laurie could find to say.

"Oh, I shall remain until the end of the Season," he assured her. "I cannot leave until Dora and I have arranged everything."

"Dora. Yes, of course." Laurie spurred abruptly ahead. She knew exactly what he was going to say, and she didn't want to hear it—not then, not ever.

There were already signs of life in the streets. Cleaners with their brushes and carts and long-handled shovels had begun the task of sweetening the city, and the early haze that hung over the distant steeples had given way to pale, clear light.

"I will stable the horses," said Tarquin as they trotted into the yard.

George was astir, however, scratching his head as he surveyed the two vacant stalls. He beamed with relief at the arrival of his employer. "I figured there'd been mischief," he said.

"A great deal of mischief, George." Tarquin dismounted, swung Laurie unceremoniously to the ground, and nodded amiably. "See to Jasper and Rainbow, will you?"

"Yes, Mr. St. John." The groom's reply was somewhat bemused as he took a full look at Laurie, her carefully coiled hair tumbling down round her shoulders, the coat and breeches grass-stained.

"Come along, Cousin Laurentia," Tarquin said, pushing open the side door.

She went ahead of him and climbed the stairs, hoping he would turn in the direction of his own room and leave her to compose herself for whatever announcement he and Dora planned to make, but he caught at her arm.

"We have shocked George to the core of his respectable soul," he observed. "You are quite compromised in his eyes, you know. He will certainly expect me to marry you now."

"That's foolish," she objected. "You can't marry both Dora and me."

"Granted, but I wasn't thinking of marrying Dora. Dora has a distinguished career ahead of her if she practises very hard to make up for the time she has wasted. She is to attend a lycée in Paris, where particular attention is paid to budding concert pianists and composers."

Laurie stared at him, open-mouthed.

"I have talked it over with her," Tarquin said, "and she is most enthusiastic. She is only seventeen, and after a year in Paris she will have blossomed into a bride fit for a duke."

"But I had planned for Dora to marry you," Laurie said at last.

"Dora assured me that both she and Clarisse had set their hearts on my marrying you."

"You don't have to marry any of us," Laurie said stiffly. "If Dora wishes for a musical career in Paris, then naturally I shall not oppose it. Clarisse will likely fall in love with Simon after all, but I can still go back to Gables. You don't have to worry about me."

"I am not in the least worried about you," he said equably, "but I am gravely concerned for the unfortunate people whose lives you will be trying to rearrange if you are left to your own devices. However, on the ranch in the Americas you can ride astride and fire off pistols to frighten the Indians."

"I do wish you would stop teasing me," Laurie said uncertainly. "I haven't the smallest desire to marry you or anybody else. I am destined to be a spinster, I believe." She broke off as a cascade of notes sounded from the music room, followed by Dora's clear soprano, fitting words to a tune she was evidently just composing, since now and then she strummed for a moment or two before continuing.

> "Once there was a heart. Stolen now.
> No need to cry.
> Once there was a man, I saw his face,
> Passing by.
> World full of people, streets wet with rain,
> When will I find that sweet thief again,
> Holding my heart in his hands?"

"I don't know the song," Tarquin said.

"I felt a poem coming on last night," Laurie admitted, blushing furiously. "I daresay that Dora woke early and—"

"Felt a tune coming on," Tarquin said. "What astonishing talents you do possess! And you will, of course, tell me that it is none of my business if I enquire the identity of the sweet thief who is holding your heart? Not, I pray, David Cornwall, for then I should really feel obliged to call him out myself."

"As a matter of fact," said Laurie, capitulating, "I was thinking of you."

"I was hoping you would say that." Tarquin pulled her closer, smiling down into her eyes. "I wonder what you are thinking now."

"That it's going to be a lovely morning," Laurie said, and the rest of her hair tumbled down as she lifted her face to his kiss.